RON WOOD... "GIMME SOME NECK"

KEITH RICHARDS
BENEFIT CONCERT

GUEST

New Barbarians

KPRI FM 106 In Association With
LARRY VALLON
Presents
THE NEW BARBARIANS
★ ★ ★ ★ ★ ★ ★ ★ ★ ★
SAN DIEGO SPORTS ARENA
SAN DIEGO, CA

1979

THIS DATE ONLY

$9.00

REFUND PRICE NO EXCHANGE

SEC   ROW   SEAT

TUESDAY
8:00 P.M.

MAJOR EVENTS
nts
 BARBARIANS
★ ★ ★ ★ ★
ENA
MICHIGAN
ARBOR, MICHIGAN
TUESDAY
8:00 P.M.

$12.50

SEC   ROW   SEAT
27   24   6

GOLD TIER

410 AD

THE BARBARIAN HORDES—LED BY ALARIC, SON OF ROTHESTEUS AND UNDISPUTED KING OF THE VISIGOTHS—SWEEP OUT OF THE GERMANIC LANDS AND THROUGH THE HOLY ROMAN EMPIRE, PILLAGING AND RAPING THE CIVILIZED LANDS, SACKING ROME ON 24 AUGUST 410 AD. OTHER BARBARIANS WERE ALSO ON THE RAMPAGE DURING THE 5TH CENTURY: THE ANGLO-SAXONS OVERRAN BRITANNIA ON THE HEELS OF THE FLEEING ROMANS IN 406, WHILE THE VANDALS INVADED SPAIN AND NORTH AFRICA BEFORE THEY TOO SACKED ROME IN 455.

1979 AD

THE NEW BARBARIANS—FRONTED BY RONNIE WOOD AND KEITH RICHARDS—ROCK AND ROLL OUT OF REHEARSALS IN SOUTHERN CALIFORNIA TO RAGE ON STAGE FOR TWO SHOWS OPENING FOR THE ROLLING STONES ON 22 APRIL AT THE OSHAWA CIVIC AUDITORIUM, CANADA. THEY THEN PARTY THROUGH THE UNITED STATES FROM ANN ARBOR, MICHIGAN, ON 24 APRIL TO SAN DIEGO, CALIFORNIA, ON 22 MAY, WITH OUTBREAKS AT NUMEROUS CONCERTS ALONG THE WAY, INCLUDING A SHOW IN MILWAUKEE THAT ENDED IN RIOTS AND SACKING THE MILWAUKEE ARENA. THE NEW BARBARIANS FORGE ON TO ENGLAND, OPENING FOR LED ZEPPELIN AT KNEBWORTH FESTIVAL ON 11 AUGUST.

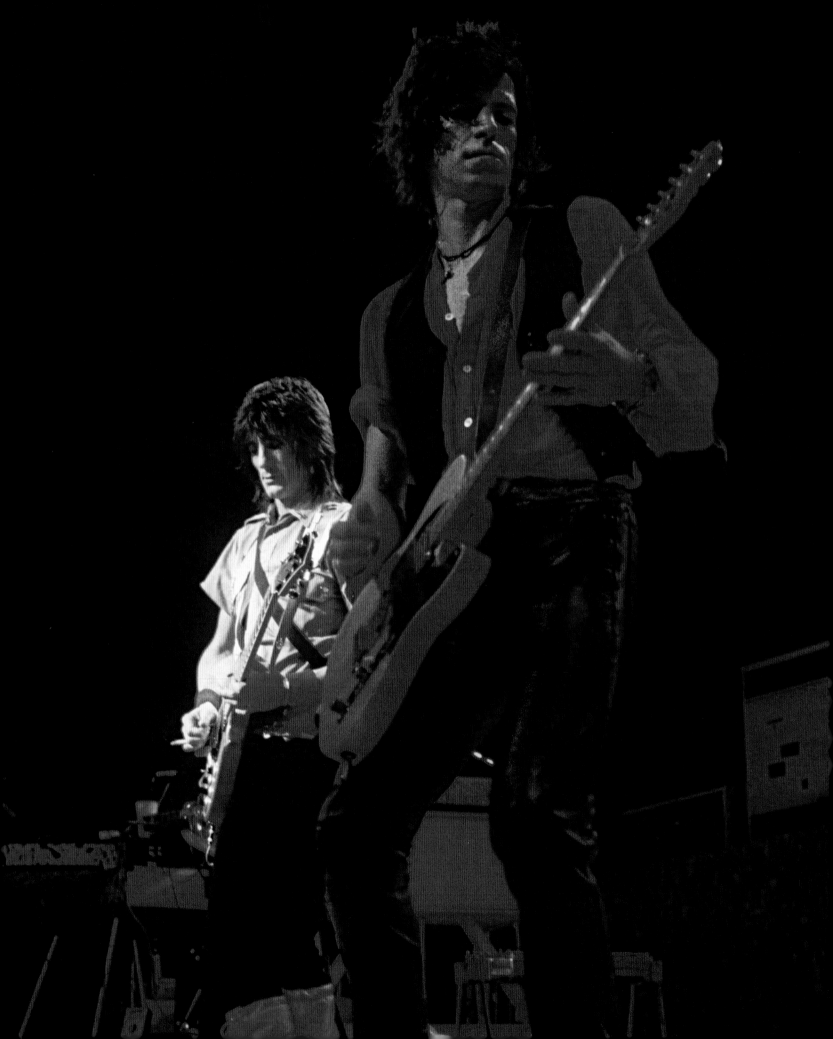

OUTLAWS, GUNSLINGERS, AND GUITARS

ROB CHAPMAN

VOYAGEUR
PRESS

CONTENTS

DEVIL'S WORK

"IDLE HANDS ARE THE DEVIL'S WORKSHOP."

— PROVERBS 16:27

Only rarely does a biblical admonition prove more true than in the practiced and calloused hands of the Rolling Stones. Ronnie Wood—on his merry way to becoming a serial offender: ex–Jeff Beck Group bassman, former Face, solo artist, newly rolled Stone, and soon-to-be grand poobah of the nouveau Barbarians—tells it best in his autobiography: "When the Stones announced that we would not tour in 1979, which sort of broke from tradition because the summer after a US tour we usually came to Europe, Charlie Watts formed a group called Rocket 88 with Ian Stewart, Alexis Korner, and Dick Morrisey. It was a boogie-woogie band that got together because the guys playing in it just loved playing. Charlie said they were having a great time, so I decided it would be fun to do something like that, and as long as I had time off from touring with the Stones, I'd get some of my mates together and go on tour with them. It was an extracurricular activity, but then touring has always been in my blood. . . . Because in those days the energy level was really high and because it was part of my thing to keep working, not stop. So I rang around and deliberately put together some risky pairings with musicians who had never played together before, or since, for that matter. Just like that we headed off on the craziest tour ever."

And so the New Barbarians were born.

Idle hands doing the devil's work played other roles in the band's pre-story as well. In a strange, roundabout way, the story of the Barbarians begins with Keith Richards' infamous drug bust in Toronto in February 1977. At the time, his arrest appeared to signal the last hurrah of the Stones: It seemed likely that Keith was about to be shepherded by the

Royal Canadian Mounted Police to a jail cell for the rest of his natural life. In the end, after 20 months of handwringing and heartache on the band's side and fire-and-brimstone speeches from self-righteous Canadian authorities, Keith was allowed to serve his sentence by enlisting both the Barbarians and the Stones into playing two charity shows in Oshawa, Canada, on 22 April 1979.

It was during the Stones' five-month-long *Some Girls* recording sessions from October 1977 and on into March 1978 that Wood found himself with time to twiddle his thumbs. So, he rounded up his own "pickup band"—which just happened to include at various moments Keith, Mick Jagger, Charlie Watts, Mick Fleetwood, Dave Mason, and Mick Taylor—and led them into studios in Paris and L.A. to cut what became his third solo album, released on 20 April 1979 as *Gimme Some Neck*. And when it came to pass that there would be no '79 European tour to follow up the Stones' '78 *Some Girls* Tour across the United States, Wood found himself with most of a year off and spare time on his hands.

So, Ronnie set in motion the Barbarians tour with Keith at his side to give the two Stones with the most insatiable appetites for gigging and jamming and having fun something worthwhile to do in society's critical eye. Again, Ronnie tells it best, writing in his autobiography: "I booked the whole tour, I was paying for it and I wanted to take my friends around in style. Mr Generous here. I got us a Boeing 727, took care of everybody luxuriously, and wound up £200,000 in debt. I'm not a businessman, but I made sure that all my mates got paid. . . . I wanted to do the whole thing proper, but after Bo Diddley said to me, 'Are you kidding? I steal the fucking place mats out of the hotel,' that's when I started to think did I really shell out for a jet? Bo kept saying, 'Man you gotta be crazy.' And maybe I was. Maybe that's why I lost £200,000 on that tour."

If the Barbarians' history was short—and largely unnoted in Stones lore—their legacy was long.

Yes, the Barbarians' tour resulted in some great music, although too little of it was officially recorded or filmed. Yes, the Barbarians were one of the greatest supergroups of all time—and one of the few that didn't end on a sour note, broken apart by acrimonious "artistic disagreements." Yes, the Barbarians helped pay Keith's debt to society, if not in full at least to even out the balance sheet, to date.

The Barbarians did more, as well. The solo album and tour gave Ronnie artistic success, standing him up firmly as a full-fledged, worthy Stone for the future.

At the same time, the Barbarians provided Keith an opportunity to refocus his life, cast out several of his demons, and find redemption in rock 'n' roll—in turn enabling the Stones themselves to survive and thrive.

And yes, it kept Ronnie, Keith, and company out of trouble during their year off.

At least sort of.

CHAPTER 1
COCKROACHES

"THERE IS SERIOUS TALK THAT THE STONES HAVE HAD IT."

— CHET FLIPPO

1976 TOUR OF EUROPE
(Opposite) The Stones' *Love You Live* album featured songs from their European tour, which included an April date in Frankfurt.

Michael Putland/Getty Images

Keith Richards' Toronto drug bust of 1977 had everything and nothing to do with the New Barbarians. From the ground-floor level, his subsequent sentence merely provided a venue for the band to debut—not that that would have been hard to come by almost anywhere had management gone asking. But from the penthouse's sweeping panoramic view, Keith's dire drug situation and ensuing resurrection became the underlying theme of the band from '77 through the end of the decade.

Details of the drug bust are old news now. At the time, however, it was the stuff of headlines. It was shocking, unbelievable, scandalous, heralding the decline of western civilization—and thus suitably titillating to Joe Citizen at home in his comfy chair before the fire with the evening paper. More importantly, though, Keef's arrest raised the specter of the dissolution of the Stones as a whole.

In early 1977, the Stones signed a four-record deal with Atlantic for an unprecedented $14 million. The contract included provisions for one live recording, so tracks were culled from the 1975 Tour of the Americas and subsequent 1976 Tour of Europe. There were so many gems that the decision was made to expand the release to a double LP, which would be *Love You Live*. But in the meantime, the Stones had

EL MO
The famous neon marquee heralding the El Mocambo Tavern.

come up short. So, the band members dutifully converged on Toronto in late February 1977 to tape two gigs slated for a neighborhood "local," the El Mocambo Tavern, to fill out the discs.

The rest of the Stones rolled in on 20 February, but Keith lagged behind, fashionably late to the party.

As the free world's most elegant reprobate, Richards was a lusty and louche Lord Byron for modern times—electrified, plugged in, and amped up. And to point his own quip about Gram Parsons back at him, Keith always had better drugs than the mafia. He was notorious and he was glorious—and to society at large, he was precipitating the fall of all that was good and decent, the destruction of civilization in person behind those mirrored aviators. So, when he finally arrived at Toronto International Airport from London on 24 February with Anita Pallenberg and their son, Marlon, in tow, it caused the usual commotion.

Pallenberg was the well-established seventh Stone (Ian Stewart being a more official sixth). And she was Keith's *éminence blonde*. Born in Rome to a German mother and Italian father, her looks and

THE SEVENTH STONE

Keith and Anita Pallenberg, who was sometimes called the seventh Stone.

Graham Wiltshire/Redferns

LOVE YOU LIVE

The Stones promote the release
of their live album *Love You Live*.

Bettmann/Getty Images

personality were the best of both nationalities: impossibly beautiful and impossibly smart, she was nothing less than a force of nature. She was at times a model, fashion designer, and movie actress—but was never a mere band groupie, despite her dalliances with Brian Jones and Mick Jagger as well as Keith. Anita Pallenberg was the sole personage who could out-Stones the Stones.

She landed in Toronto with twenty-eight pieces of luggage—which naturally piqued the Canadian customs agents' curiosity. Deep inside one of those bags, officials unearthed ten grams of what they called "high-quality hashish." In another, they found a spoon that, according to their lab tests, contained traces of heroin. Pallenberg was arrested, then immediately released on a "promise-to-appear" notice. According to *Rolling Stone* magazine's Chet Flippo, who rushed to Toronto to cover the biggest story of the year along with global media from the *New York Times* to the *Times* of London, "a

"THE MOUNTIES ALWAYS GET THEIR MAN."

close Stones source said that Keith was 'groggy at the airport and, when their luggage was being searched, actually thought that it was record company people who had come to the airport to help him. He had no idea it was the RCMP.'"

The Mounties were hot on the scent and not finished with Richards. Just weeks earlier, on 12 January, the Aylesbury Crown Court in London had tried him for yet another highly publicized drug bust, acquitting him of possession of LSD charges, but finding him guilty of possessing cocaine; he was fined £750 and assessed another £250 in court fees. And he was slapped on the wrist by Judge Lawrence Verney, who loudly warned that one more conviction would lead him straight to prison.

Three days after Pallenberg's arrest at the airport, fifteen Royal Canadian Mounted Police and Ontario provincial policemen staged what Flippo described as a "lightning-fast, Entebbe-like raid" on Toronto's Stones headquarters, the Harbour Castle Hotel. Flippo reported rumors that someone in the hotel had tipped off the Mounties, yet still the raid required some 45 minutes of stomping through the many corridors and suites of the Stones' roped-off floors of extra "floater" rooms before they located Keith's suite, booked under the alias Mr. K. Redlings.

In one of the several bathrooms of his suite, the police found an ounce of what they later said was "high-quality heroin with a street value of $4,000." Living up to their own legend, the Mounties always get their man.

Richards was arrested on the spot, but soon released on a $1,000 bond. Pallenberg was re-arrested, then released without bond. And their passports were seized, so they couldn't flee Canada until their cases were settled.

Pallenberg arrived in court on 4 March, plead guilty to possessing heroin and cannabis, was fined, and released. Ultimately, she was the little fish caught in the net. The big catch was Keith, who was scheduled to appear on 7 March in Toronto court at Old City Hall. The

BUSTED

Accompanied by his press agent, Paul Wasserman (left), Keith Richards makes his way through the press and fans into Toronto's Old City Hall in March 1977 to face a charge of possessing heroin for the purpose of trafficking. A second charge of possessing cocaine was added later.

Keith Richards Ron Bull/*Toronto Star*/Getty Images

charge: possession of heroin for the purpose of trafficking. The penalty: seven years to life.

In the meantime, Richards was slapped with yet another charge. The Mounties' lab found that a further substance seized from his hotel room was cocaine. The future looked less than bright.

Chet Flippo's coverage of the Toronto brouhaha was brilliant first-person gonzo journalism, capturing that peculiar paranoia at the heart of the great 1970s battle waged between the pillars of society and the barbarians at the gates, best personified by the Rolling Stones in general and Richards in particular. Band consiglieri, lawyers, security men, handlers, and hangers-on worked overtime negotiating with the police and obfuscating the situation with the

"WHAT DISAPPOINTS ME WAS THAT NOT ONE OF THEM WAS WEARING A PROPER MOUNTIES UNIFORM WHEN THEY BURST INTO MY HOTEL ROOM. THEY WERE ALL IN ANORAKS WITH DROOPY MOUSTACHES AND BALD HEADS. . . . I'D HAVE WOKEN UP A LOT QUICKER IF I'D SEEN THE RED TUNIC AND SMOKEY BEAR HAT."

— KEITH RICHARDS

press. Caught up in the midst of the maelstrom, even Flippo himself suffered a brief breakdown.

Along with the potential end of civilization as a whole, the real news here was writ in Flippo's *Rolling Stone* headline of 7 April 1977: "Stone's Future Cloudy." In his various dispatches from the front lines, he wrote that "there is serious talk that the Stones have had it." Canadian shadowmen lurked around corners; unmarked cars followed the Stones everywhere. Flippo finally wormed his way through the Stones' bodyguards and got an audience with Mick Jagger and Charlie Watts. In one instance, Jagger poo-pooed rumors of the band's demise as "rubbish" and "journalistic claptrap." In another, he was in a panic, "desperate and depressed." (Watts, however, remained cool and calm, unflappable and aloof.)

Yet the show must go on, whatever the future held. As *Creem* magazine reported, "Throughout the week, they rehearsed from midnight 'til dawn in a seedy room next to an all-night Gulf gas station. Everything was low-profile, including the food, supplied exclusively by a café down the road that specialized in soggy ham and cheese sandwiches. Night after night they ran through songs they hadn't played onstage in years, like 'Around and Around' and 'Little Red Rooster'; songs they hadn't played onstage before like 'Crazy Mama', 'Memory Motel' and 'Dance Little Sister'; and two new tunes. Even at rehearsals the spontaneous atmosphere was contagious."

And still, despite the furor of Keith's drug bust, the concerts themselves were kept hush-hush.

UNPHASED

Mick stays cool as a camera flashes at a promotional event in New York City.

Three hundred lucky listeners of Toronto's CHUM radio station had answered the question, "Why I Want To Party With The Stones" and won tickets to a surprise secret evening. Among the winning entries were comments that made Jagger, Richards, and gang scratch their heads or guffaw out loud, including, "I would like to go to the Rolling Stones' party because I really like their music, especially 'Stairway to Heaven'" and "I'm the real Mick Jagger and I'd like to meet the sono-fabitch who thinks he's me." It was not an auspicious beginning.

The venue for the concerts—the El Mocambo Tavern—was a cramped, low-ceilinged neighborhood nightclub just large enough to swing a cat in; it was a far throw from the arenas and stadiums the band had been playing for years. In fact, it would be the band's first club gig since playing a Bristol, England, date—on 13 November 1964. Flippo reported that at 6 p.m. on Friday night, 4 March 1977, the 300 contest winners met at CHUM, filed onto buses, and without being told of their destination, were driven to the tavern, whose marquee announced a concert by Canadian rockers April Wine. But curiously, policemen surrounded the venue, hovering like vultures.

April Wine opened the show (and would release their own *Live at the El Mocambo* from the date). Then came a band known only as the Cockroaches.

"Amazingly, the crowd still didn't know who was going to be playing," remembers crew member Johnny Starbuck. "April Wine actually did do a set, and then there was a break and the crowd hung around for whatever was going to be next. When the Stones were ready, we went up the back stairs and through the kitchen and had the audience lights turned completely off. It was fucking dark and all you could see was the red lights on the amps and the lit ends of cigarettes. Me and [fellow crew members] Gary Schultz and Chuch Magee, carrying flashlights, walked the band, all holding each other's hands in single file through the edge of the crowd, and got them up on stage. You could just feel how excited the crowd was because it really was still dark enough to not be sure who it was that was taking the stage. 'Who are the Cockroaches, anyway?'

"When the band was ready, we shot our flashlight beams at the lighting guy and the lights came on and the Rolling Stones were off and running. The people in front were right at Mick Jagger's feet and the people in the very back of the club couldn't have been more than thirty feet away. The looks on everyone's faces were priceless. They couldn't believe their luck."

The Stones—filled out by Billy Preston on keyboards and percussionist Ollie Brown—kickstarted the show with "Route 66," traveling back in time to their roots. And the atmosphere was pure roadhouse as well: "Everyone in the crowd was dancing on tables and standing on chairs with wine and beer spilling over everybody. Everyone was lighting up joints even though the whole building was surrounded by cops to keep the peace outside," Ronnie remembered in his autobiography. Jagger even did the honors of the last call: "Last orders, please!" he said. "The more you drink, the more we get."

As Keith remembered the shows, "The minute I got onstage, it felt like just another Sunday gig at the Crawdaddy. It immediately felt the same. . . . Everybody's going around talking doom and disaster,

4 MARCH 1977
The media catches a glimpse of Ronnie the night before the secret gig at the El Mocambo. John Mahler/*Toronto Star* via Getty Images

EL MOCAMBO

El Mocambo was a legendary venue in the Toronto music scene even before the Stones billed themselves as "The Cockroaches" and played a surprise club show. First opened as a tavern on 23 March 1948, El Mocambo mainly operated as a dining hall and didn't even feature live music until a few months later.

After a change of ownership in 1972, the venue shifted its focus to what it's now known for: blues and rock. Up-and-coming artists such as U2, Elvis Costello, and Tom Waits were among the acts to grace the club's stage. After the infamous Rolling Stones show, bigger headliners (Blondie, the Ramones) played before the club again shifted focus—local acts became the main bookings at the club.

"TORONTO WITHOUT THE EL MOCAMBO? IT JUST DOESN'T EXIST."

Since 1986, the club has cycled through a series of closings and reopenings. In November 2014, El Mocambo's doors were going to be locked for good until local CEO Michael Wekerle stepped in with an offer at the eleventh hour. He pledged that the El Mo wasn't finished yet: "Toronto without the El Mocambo? It just doesn't exist."

The first few weeks of 2016 finally brought a stir of activity at the shuttered venue—the iconic palm tree sign came down in January to be restored, only the second time it got a refresh since it was installed in 1948. As of this writing, it remains to be determined when the latest reincarnation of El Mocambo will come to life. "I want to give the kids a chance to look up and say, 'I'm going to play the El Mocambo,'" Wekerle said after his purchase in 2014. "That's what it's all about."

"WHO ARE THE COCKROACHES, ANYWAY?"

and we're up onstage at the El Mocambo and we never felt better. I mean, we sounded GREAT. People were down, asking *Is this the end of the Rolling Stones?* . . . In a way, these things always bring you closer together because you've got to deal with them. What happens to me affects the whole band."

On the second night, Keith, looking "gaunt and unshaven but occasionally smiling," as Flippo reported from ringside, led the band off with "Honky Tonk Women." The Stones were even better this evening, playing with sound and fury. The show was simply "magnificent," in Flippo's one-word summation.

In the wings was one special guest—Margaret Trudeau, the 28-year-old wife of the prime minister of Canada, Pierre Trudeau. And she was thoroughly enjoying herself. Starbuck remembered:

SOUVENIR
Rita Bédard—Keith's "blind angel"—took this snapshot of Richards at the Harbour Castle Hotel in Toronto. Her friend, Curt Angeledes, focused and aimed the camera for Rita. Rita Bédard/ courtesy Curt Angeledes

LOVE YOU LIVE

Featuring cuts taken from the El Mocambo shows on side 3, *Love You Live* was released on 23 September 1977.

"She was in the dressing room—actually it was a downstairs part of the nightclub that was closed to the public and just used for the band's dressing room—and Billy Preston, who didn't know who she was, kept telling her to dash off and get him 'Another gin and tonic, love.' That was a fucking riot.

"During the show, my spot was right next to stage-right alongside Billy so I could do the mixing of the keyboards and send a stereo feed to the house mixer. The place was so small and the stage was so tiny that I was within arm's reach of the band. Margaret Trudeau sat next to me on my bench and kept pulling joints out of her pocket and lighting them and taking a hit and then handing it to me and I would take a hit and hand it to Billy, who would take a hit and keep passing across the stage 'til it got to Keith on the other side of the stage. Man, what a night!"

That was just the start of things. Trudeau also had a suite at the Harbour Castle Hotel and hosted an aftershow party that ran until the wee hours. It turned out that "Honky Tonk Women" was too apt of an opening song—serving as a sort of unintended taunt to all of Canada. Suddenly, Keith was no longer headline news, but the Stones still were. Read one newspaper banner all the way across the pond in old Blighty, "The First Lady Who Got Turned On By The Stones."

As Flippo noted, the band came to Canada for a week, disrupted the entire country, created an international incident thanks to Keith, and was now on the verge of toppling the government. Not bad for a week's work.

After the El Mo shows, the Stones quickly made their exit from Canada, Margaret Trudeau on their heels. Keith was left behind.

With time again on his hands and trying to keep himself sane, Keith went on 12–13 March to Toronto's Sounds Interchange Studios—where the band had rehearsed for the El Mocambo sessions—and picked up his guitar. He recorded a long, rambling, heartfelt set of country covers inspired by his friendship with and musical tuition under Gram Parsons. Included were Johnny Paycheck and Bobby Austin's "Apartment #9" on which Keith played piano; Dallas Frazier's "Say It's Not You," which was a hit for George Jones; Glenn Sutton's "She Still Comes Around," which Jerry Lee Lewis covered; and, with Ian Stewart on piano, "Worried Life Blues" as cut by Major "Big Maceo" Merriweather and Tampa Red. The studio had multiple engineers to keep pace with Keith's sleepless energy; he also wrote "Rotten Roll"—the working title for "Before They Make Me Run"—during the sessions, Gary Schultz remembers. And Keith recorded—perhaps with apprehension about his future—a particularly soulful, doleful take of Merle Haggard's jailhouse lament "Sing Me Back Home."

The day after the recording sessions, Keith was back in court. He was handed his passport, but it was not until April Fool's Day that he could finally secure a U.S. visa and exit Canada at long last. He went to Philadelphia, then on to the town of Paoli, where he entered a three-week-long heroin cure under Dr. Meg Patterson using the supposedly painless Black Box treatment: Fitted with electrodes, he was given small electric shocks that released endorphins to counteract withdrawal symptoms.

During this same time in mid-March, the rest of the Stones met in New York City to discuss the band's future. Not knowing what would happen with Keith, they could only guess at their own destiny.

For the next 19 months, Keith's life was a mess of legal wranglings, withdrawal treatments, psychiatric evaluations, and psychotherapy sessions. Finally, after various false starts, a trial date was scheduled for 23 October 1978.

Keith moved to Cherry Hill, New Jersey, within the 25-mile radius of Philadelphia mandated by the U.S. visa his lawyers were able to negotiate for him, and he and Jagger mixed the *Love You Live*

MOVING THE GOODS

In the bad old '70s, shuffling gear from gig to gig was an art, not the science it is today. Crew member Johnny Starbuck remembers the shenanigans they went through to get equipment to and from the El Mo shows:

"Gary Schultz and I were finishing up a Billy Preston tour and the last shows were in New England. We had Billy's gear flown as excess baggage (can you believe that we used to be able to get away with that?) and flew from L.A. to Boston and rented a Hertz rental truck with Billy's manager's credit card at the price of a local rental. We then picked up Billy's gear and did six or seven shows around New England, and then took the truck across the border into Canada to go to Toronto for the Rolling Stones El Mocambo rehearsals.

"Keep in mind that a local truck rental means you're going to have it a few days and turn it in at the place where you rented it. What happened was we used it around New England for two or three weeks and then took it to Canada, where it sat in the parking lot of the rehearsal studio for the next month or so.

"After the El Mocambo show, Billy Preston's manager wanted to know how his equipment was going to get back to Los Angeles. So, what the hell, Gary and I said that for a couple of grand we'd take it back in the truck.

"A few days later after dropping the equipment off at Billy's house in Topanga Canyon, we waited til the local Hertz truck rental office was closed and drove the truck there and parked it in front of the door and dropped the keys through the mail slot. We figured they'd be so happy that their truck turned up that we'd never hear from them again.

"And we didn't."

"THE LOOKS ON EVERYONE'S FACES WERE PRICELESS. THEY COULDN'T BELIEVE THEIR LUCK."

recordings at the City of Brotherly Love's Sigma Sound Studios. The double-LP was released on 23 September 1977 featuring cover art by Andy Warhol—with Jagger's unsolicited painterly additions.

Even with the Toronto trial hanging over Keith's head like a guillotine blade and the Stones' future still uncertain, the band began recording a new album in Paris. From October through 2 March of the new year—with time out for the holidays—they settled in at Studio Pathé Marconi EMI in Boulogne-Billancourt on the outskirts of Paris to cut the tracks that would become *Some Girls*. The band was inspired, renewed, energized. As Keith said, "The bust in Canada . . . was a real watershed—or WaterGATE—for me. I'd gone to jail, been cleaned up, done my cure, and I'd wanted to come back and prove there was some difference . . . some . . . some reason for this kind of suffering."

Some Girls was released on 16 June 1978 to near-universal praise. As Keith said, it was "like we'd been away for a bit, and we came back with a bang." The new LP was a worldwide hit, rejuvenating the band when they needed it most as they set off on the '78 *Some Girls* Tour. No Canadian dates were on the schedule.

Fans and critics alike echoed Nick Tosches' exuberant review of *Some Girls* in *Circus*: "The men that made *It's Only Rock 'n' Roll* and *Black and Blue* seemed not to be the Rolling Stones, but rather a group of chic salon entertainers who had sold their souls to Satan in exchange for an introduction to Sterling St. Jacques. They had achieved the satisfaction they had so loudly and gloriously sought more than ten years before, and it resembled a lightly buttered croissant. It was over. . . . [But] I played the album, and forgave and forgot the past sins of the Rolling Stones; for *Some Girls* not only asks forgiveness for those sins—it demands it, in a most surly way."

On 23 October, Keith returned to Toronto for the trial at the New Court House. The prosecution dropped the cocaine charge, as Richards pled guilty to a reduced charge of heroin possession and agreed to forego a jury trial in exchange for the other charges being dropped, as Flippo reported. His attorney, Austin Cooper, blamed Keith's heroin addiction on artistic angst: "Richards is an intensely creative person who is often wracked with emotional pain. . . . His everyday life can be hell." Cooper compared him to tortured French poet Charles Baudelaire, Vincent van Gogh, Sylvia Plath, Judy Garland, Billie Holiday, and F. Scott Fitzgerald, stating that art is created from "pieces of the shattered self." After testimony was presented concerning Keith's exemplary rehabilitation, Cooper concluded, "The public interest would best be served by allowing him to prop up his sagging personal life, to continue his musical work and to continue his treatment."

As poignant as the testimony may have been, it was the steadfast presence of a Stones fan at the court proceedings that may have finally tipped the scales of justice in Keith's favor. Rita Bédard was "a young girl who melted the judge's heart with her love for the Stones," Ronnie explained in his autobiography. And she was blind, which inspired Judge Lloyd Graburn in his sentence.

Keith has told the story of his "blind angel" many times over the years: "This blind chick in Montreal would go to every Stones gig she could. I met her—way before the bust—and I'd make sure she'd get rides, hook her up with the truck drivers, 'Hey, look, she's blind, no monkey business, boys. Just make sure she's going to get there, because if she's gonna be thumbing down the road blind as a bat, eventually what could happen to her?' When I got popped, evidently she went to the judge handling the case, knocked on his door one night and told him the story. I think he probably had a brief from above, 'We want this case settled, out of here,' and he had this blinding flash of inspiration to sentence me to play a benefit concert for the blind."

On 24 October 1978, Judge Graburn handed down his judgment: Keith was sentenced to a year probation, continued heroin treatment, and to play the benefit concert for the Canadian National Institute for the Blind within six months. The Crown would appeal, demanding incarceration. But for now, Keith was free.

SOME GIRLS
From October 1977 through February 1978, the Stones recorded the tracks that would become *Some Girls* at Studio Pathé Marconi EMI in Paris. The LP became a global hit, and the band set off on the '78 *Some Girls* Tour—which did not include any Canadian shows.

"THEY ARE REALLY OUT TO MAKE ROCK & ROLL ILLEGAL."

— KEITH RICHARDS

In the following months, Keith could finally speak out publicly about the bust—and speak out he did, his comments ranging from humorous to astringent.

"Thinking about the bust," he told *Melody Maker*, "what disappoints me was that not one of them was wearing a proper Mounties uniform when they burst into my hotel room. They were all in Anoraks with droopy moustaches and bald heads. Real WEEDS, the whole lot of 'em, all just after their picture in the paper. Fifteen of 'em, round me bed, trying to wake me up. I'd have woken up a lot quicker if I'd seen the red tunic and Smokey Bear hat."

About his trial, though, all he said was, "It was very boring having to sit there and listen to it all."

And he felt like he was a scapegoat, a pawn in a larger game. Margaret Trudeau's rumored tryst with one of the Stones—most often hinted to be Jagger—had incensed the Canadian prosecutors' determination to see him do time: "I end up feeling that I have to pay for the Rape of Canada."

Most of all, however, he saw his repeated arrests and trials as part of a concerted war against rock 'n' roll. He told *Creem*, "On one hand, they say the Rolling Stones and rock musicians in general are corrupting the kids, but if they just left us alone and didn't come looking for drugs then nobody would know if we had a drug problem or not. It's all just a camouflage." In his mind, he was taking the rap for all rock 'n' rollers; as he told *Rolling Stone*, "They are really out to make rock & roll illegal."

Concerning his sentence, he gave thanks to his blind angel and was ready to grab his guitar again. As he joshed with *Melody Maker*, "How can you appear in front of the blind? But whoever I have to play for, the blind, deaf or bubonic plague victims, I'll do what I've always done anyway."

A PICTURE OF STRESS
(Opposite) Keith Richards is grilled at a press conference shortly after being arrested in Toronto. AP Photo/Blaise Edwards

CHAPTER 2
SOME NECK

"I'VE GOT MY OWN ALBUM TO DO."

— VARIOUS FACES

STONE ALONE
(Opposite) Ronnie Wood up close, from the batch of
promotional photos released to the media for the launch
of *Gimme Some Neck* on 20 April 1979. Columbia Records/CBS

Gimme Some Neck (Above left) promotional wooden coin.
Curt Angeledes collection

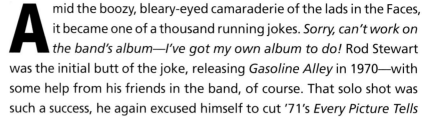

Amid the boozy, bleary-eyed camaraderie of the lads in the Faces, it became one of a thousand running jokes. *Sorry, can't work on the band's album—I've got my own album to do!* Rod Stewart was the initial butt of the joke, releasing *Gasoline Alley* in 1970—with some help from his friends in the band, of course. That solo shot was such a success, he again excused himself to cut '71's *Every Picture Tells a Story*, and then '72's *Never a Dull Moment*. Ronnie Lane exited from the band in '73 to make his own albums. And Ronnie Wood made the joke public when he titled his '74 solo debut *I've Got My Own Album to Do*. (Ian "Mac" McLagan would eventually follow suit with *Troublemaker* in '79, but that would be part of the New Barbarians' story.)

The joke was a good 'un—good, that is, until Stewart's solo shots became more successful than the band's own albums and ultimately helped hasten the Faces' demise.

Wood brought that humor along to the Stones. The five-month-long *Some Girls* recording sessions at Paris' Studio Pathé Marconi EMI that ran on and off from 10 October 1977 through 2 March 1978 were refreshingly fruitful and prolific. In the end, the sessions provided ten tracks that made up the band's comeback album—as well as impetus, inspiration, and a studio setup that they'd return to for *Emotional Rescue*. And somewhere, somehow, Woody found spare moments there to cut his own solo album at the same time.

Having the Stones available to watch his back on the album was handy. Jagger added backing vocals on a track; Keith played guitar on one cut and sang on a couple others; Watts played drums on every track save one. It was akin to cutting a Faces solo album all over again. And in the end, the vibe of *Gimme Some Neck* was more akin to *Exile on Main St.* than *Some Girls*; perhaps the Stones were getting their rocks off on Woody's solo album and channeling their dance, disco, and vintage R&B into the band's album.

Woody also worked his charm and magic and pulled more of his fabled pals into the studio. Mick Fleetwood drummed on the one track Watts wasn't available for while Jim Keltner added percussion on two others. Dave Mason played acoustic guitar on one tune, and Robert "Pops" Powell of the Crusaders added the bassline throughout. Sometime-Stone Bobby Keys honked the sax. And former Face McLagan overdubbed keyboards at Cherokee Studios in L.A., near Mac's new Malibu beach home and Woody's Mandeville Canyon house.

I'VE GOT MY OWN ALBUM TO DO!

(Opposite) It was just one of thousands of jokes among the Faces, but it lost some of its humor after Rod Stewart's *Gasoline Alley* became a huge hit, eventually precipitating the end of the band.

In the producer's chair was Roy Thomas Baker, who had started at Decca Records when he was just 14. Since then, he had led sessions by David Bowie, Hawkwind, Queen, the Cars, and Journey. Baker was ideal for Woody: He knew when to step in and guide production, and when to keep his hands to himself. With Wood and Co., he let proceedings proceed, simply capturing the garage-rock sound on tape.

"DON'T MAKE IT TOO 10CC."

— RONNIE WOOD

Ronnie explained to *Rolling Stone*: "Roy had heard the earlier records, and the first thing he said was, 'We don't want to make a second-rate Stones album, and we don't want your vocals to go down the way they did before.' He always seemed so unimpressed with what I was doing that I began hearing myself more critically, too. All I wanted on those first records was a one-off, back-room sound. This time, I got a back-room sound produced to the full. But I refuse to get too refined about making records. I like the earthy approach to rock & roll."

The engineer was Geoff Workman, "a Liverpudlian lad who's real down to earth and is magic with the old faders," as Woody told *Trouser Press*. Together, they worked on the album with a simple mantra: "Don't make it too 10cc," as Ronnie said.

The result was a pipeful of shambolic rock 'n' roll kicking off with what could have been Ronnie's theme song—"Worry No More." The tune had been penned by Texas wildman rock 'n' roller Jerry Lynn Williams, whose songs would be covered by everyone from B.B. King to Eric Clapton over the years. It was Johnny Starbuck who earlier introduced Williams to Ronnie and Keith, and Williams had given Woody a tape of demos a year earlier. As Ron said: "He came to the session and I said, 'Since you're here, can I do that song of yours, "Worry No More"?' He said sure. I asked him if he'd recorded it and he said he hadn't. Even better." Williams backed Ron's vocals with rollicking honky-tonk piano. It was the perfect album opener, replete with a devil-may-care chorus:

When the devil comes around
He's gonna be knock-knock-knock-knocking
Knocking at your front door
You gotta go out and greet him
Greet him with a smile
Sayin', "Devil, I don't worry no more"

SOLO CAREER

Ronnie Wood is best known as a Face and Stone, but he's also established a prolific solo career. His early solo albums include *I've Got My Own Album to Do*, *Now Look*, and the film soundtrack made with Ronnie Lane, *Mahoney's Last Stand*.

Let me tell you ~~bout~~ someone who aint
~~who is unpleas~~ pleasant to meet
You wouldn't offer her a ~~back~~ seat
Just 'cos her father a vicar
Who is full of ~~pulpit~~
There is no one sicker
~~more~~ full of S. H. one T.

SHE LOOKS REAL CUTE WHEN SHE PUTS IN THE BOOT
A NIGHT TIME SLICKER – AN A.R. LICKER
A C.O.C. TEASER – AN ICE CREAM ~~SQUEEZER~~
~~AN A.R. LICKER – A C.O.C. TEAZER~~
HER C.U.N. – REALLY DO YOU IN
~~THATS WHY I SAY F.U.~~ – TRY THIS FOR SIZE
BUT DONT YOU F.U.C. HER – IF I WOULDN'T TOUCH HER WITH MINE
WELL SHE WENT TO CALIFORNIA TURNED ~~EVERYBODY~~ OFF
ONE OF THOSE ^STRANGE PEOPLE YOU JUST LOVE TO HATE
SHE USED TO MAKE EVERYONE CREAM
IN HER ICE BLUE JEANS AND ~~THAT~~ JAR OF VASELINE

CHORUS —— BLAH BLAH BLAH – ~~A C.O.C. TEAZER~~ REALLY DO YOU IN
THATS WHY I SAY F.U. – TRY THIS FOR SIZE

SOLO

VERSE
SHE LOOKS REAL CUTE WHEN SHE PUTS IN THE BOOT
A NIGHT TIME SLICKER – AN A.R. LICKER
A C.O.C. TEAZER – AN ICE CREAM ~~SQUEEZER~~
HER C.U.N. – REALLY DO YOU IN
DONT YOU TRY TO F.U.C. HER – IF I WONT TOUCH HER WITH MINE

Well she went to California
turned everybody off.
She sure have nice way
of messin things up

Chorus.
  She looks real cute
  when she puts in the boot
  a night time slicker
  an A.R. licker
  a C.O.C. teaser
  an ice cream squeezer
  thats why i say F.U.
  try this fw size
        SOLO

one of those people
you just love to hate

He thinks this see
everything
there is to try.

Let me tell you 'bout someone
who's unpleasant to meet,
You wouldn't offer her a back seat
just cos her fathers a vicar
dont mean there's no one sicker
You can take it from me
(& she's full of S.H. one J
(He is full of pulpit

Ron Wood goes for the neck!

Ron Wood, along with some old mates of his and producer Roy Thomas Baker, wraps his fingers around the pulse of rock. Includes a blistering new Dylan song ("Seven Days") and ten more grabbers.

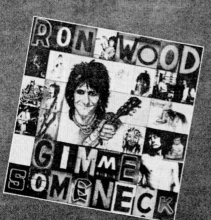

Ron Wood. "GIMME SOME NECK." His new solo album on Columbia Records and Tapes.

Ronnie then pulled out any stops that remained on his own "Breakin' My Heart," which was one of the best songs on the album. Or at least the loudest.

This was followed by a 42-second interlude of the traditional blues "Delia," Woody playing solo Dobro. The ages-old song told the sorrowful saga of 14-year-old Delia Green who was shot and killed by 15-year-old Mose Houston on Christmas Day 1900 in Savannah, Georgia, and then buried in an unmarked grave. Ronnie echoed the playing of the immortal Blind Willie McTell's 1949 version.

From there, it was more stock-in-trade rock 'n' roll: Wood's own "Buried Alive," "Come to Realise," and "Infekshun."

"WE DON'T WANT TO MAKE A SECOND-RATE STONES ALBUM."

— RONNIE WOOD

British rock critic Nick Kent would savage the album in *New Musical Express*—while apologizing profusely to "nice bloke" Woody along the way. Kent labeled "Buried Alive" and side B's "F.U.C. Her" as "puerile misogyny best left in the notebook after that inevitable night of jaded partying." What was Kent—one of the hippest, hottest writers around—expecting? Wood was central to the Faces and Stones ethos that had made their mark with *masterpieces* of misogyny, including the Faces' down-on-her-knees anthem "Stay With Me" and the Stones' "Stray Cat Blues," "Brown Sugar," "Star Fucker," "Some Girls"—the list goes on.

Ronnie's lyrics may have been rock 'n' roll doggerel, but he was a Shakespeare with a Strat, a poet when it came to crafting down-and-dirty rock 'n' roll riffs. The album was overflowing with gutsy grinds

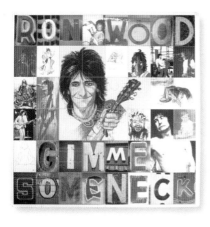

GIMME SOME NECK
Ronnie's own stylish artwork graced the cover and sleeve of the album. As Stanley Clarke remembers, "Ron Wood was a great painter. I was at his house with John Belushi [during rehearsals] and I cracked a joke, I said, 'Man you should just stop playing the guitar and do this!' He cracked up."

. . . WITH A LITTLE HELP FROM HIS MATES
(Opposite) As with the Faces' solo albums, Ronnie's side project always had some assistance from a stellar cast of mates, as this magazine advertisement heralding the arrival of *Gimme Some Neck* prominently noted. Voyageur Press collection

COME TO REALISE

SHE TOLD ME SHE MAY AS WELL SLUMBER ALONE

I DONT KNOW WHERE THE WOMAN GOT THIS IDEA FROM

KNOWN HER FOR YEARS NEVER DID ME NO WRONG

WHY SHE HARDLY GAVE ME TIME TO SLEEP

SHE WAS HOT

ARE YOU UNDER ENDOWED OR IS THAT A PENCIL

IN YOUR POCKET

IF THAT AINT A PROBLEM BOY - THEN WHATS YOUR EXCUSE

DONT BE BASHFUL YOU CAN CONFIDE IN ME,

I'VE KNOWN YOU FOR LONG ENOUGH TO SAY

ASK I DONT BITE - ASK ME IS IT EASIER FOR SOME

IS IT SOONER SAID THAN DONE - ISN'T IT

OVER BEFOR ITS BEGUN? 1st LINE

SEEMS TO ME THAT YOUR FAILING IS CAUSED BY

OTHER THAN THE SAME OLD LINE SOMETHING -

EXCUSE AGAIN

I MUST HAVE HAD TOO MUCH TO DRINK

DO I GET YOU OFF OR DO YOU HYPE IT - WHEN I DO IT -

DO YOU LIKE IT

WHY DID SHE SAY TO ME JUST WHEN IT STRUCK

HER

I'LL STICK IT BEHIND MY EAR + SMOKE IT LATER

WAS THERE ANYONE ELSE THERE - MAYBE IT WAS THE WRONG

WASN'T IT BETTER SHE SAID SHES THAT A THAT ONE

WELL

- TEN GALLON HAT OR ARE YOU ENJOYING THE WELL

THE SHOW

[MIDDLE - SEEMS TO ME ----

GOOD   ALMOST   TELL ME   ALMOST   ASK ME
GET YOU   "   AM I   "   EASIER
DO IT   COME   HYPE   LOVE   BETTER
                         DO IT   ALMOST

I'm lost and I'm lonely
I'm outa of mind
Pouring rain
Never again
Humble and helpless and hunger for you
If there could be a next time
I promise I'll stand by you
Wastin away - nothing to say
forgive me for today.
I knew it was all my fault
to let the bad man in me
?

Only the blind can tell that
I'm lookin for you
Only ~~from~~ heartaches -
can we learn
that ~~can tell~~ I'm waitin

MANUSCRIPT FOR "LOST AND LONELY"
Ronnie's working lyrics manuscript. Matt Lee collection

and lowdown grooves. And Woody's solo in "Breakin' My Heart" alone was a masterpiece—funky, far out, and not stuck and spinning mud in the usual blues-rock rut.

Billboard magazine echoed this, saying the album was "packed with biting rock'n'roll energy. . . . Most cuts are fast and uptempo." *People*, despite panning the overall product, praised its "considerable roadhouse rock energy."

On songs such as "Come To Realise" and "We All Get Old," Ronnie hit a different stride: It was as if the extra space within the calmer tempo gave him more opportunity to stretch out, both lyrically and melodically. These two tunes were diamonds among the rough.

The best was still to come, though, leading off the flipside.

Ronnie had met Bob Dylan back in '76 when the band dropped in on Eric Clapton, who was cutting his album *No Reason to Cry* at Shangri-La Studios, former studio for the group the Band near Zuma Beach in Malibu, not far from Dylan's own home. Wood had been playing on the album, too, but this was a night off. In his autobiography, he detailed their meeting: "I was hanging out with some friends on Sunset Strip, at the Roxy or the Whiskey or somewhere like that, and Eric got hold of me by phone to say, 'You'll never guess who's in the studio tonight.'

"YOU CAN HAVE THIS ONE, WOODY."

— BOB DYLAN

"He continued, 'Dylan. He's down here playing bass on one of your songs.' I said, 'Fuck, I'm coming out.'"

Ronnie went on: "I'd first met Bob at a Faces party in New York just after I did my first solo album in 1974. I really wanted people to appreciate my album, especially musicians like Bob, but never imagined that he'd know it.

"No one at the party recognized him. He just blended into the scene. And I know that some of the people there thought he was a photographer. Well, he wriggled his way through the crowd and suddenly there he was, standing in front of me, and the first thing he said was, 'I love your album.'

"That blew me away. It made me think that I must be doing something right. We spoke for five minutes or so, until Peter Grant came up to us and announced, 'Hi, I manage Led Zeppelin.'

"Bob looked at him and shot back, 'Hey, I don't come to you with my problems.'

"The next time I saw him was that night in L.A. I dashed down to Shangri-La and ended up spending two days there, hanging out with Bob. We played music all night, and all through the next day too. Whenever we took a break, Bob would disappear with some girl who had a broken leg.

"Shangri-La was a bordello back in its heyday. A hazy maze of winding corridors converted into a recording studio, strange smells and little bedrooms where you could crash. Someone showed me which room I could have, and when I finally got to bed all my blankets were gone. With my best detective instincts, I scoured the room. The window was open and curtains were blowing in the breeze. It was easy to conclude that someone had nicked my blankets and escaped through the window.

"When I looked out the window, I could see way off in the distance a little tent pitched in a field. On further investigation, I discovered that's where Bob was giving the girl with the broken leg some gypsy loving. But, not only had he made off with the wounded bird, he'd made off with my blankets.

THE BARBARIAN'S KISS

"Ronnie Wood never said no to anybody." So remembers Ernie Selgado, Ronnie's studio hand at Cherokee Studio during the recording of *Gimme Some Neck*. And because of this, after finishing his solo album, Ronnie ended up playing slide guitar in an odd place—on Kiss' Gene Simmons' 1978 solo album.

Selgado: "One night after Chuch and I had taken all the guitars and amps and accessories out of the studio at Cherokee, Gene Simmons, who was recording in Studio B, came by to ask Ronnie if he could lay down some slide guitar on one of his songs. Ronnie said, 'Sure'—but he didn't have any of his guitars. Gene said, 'No problem,' he had guitar. But there was still no slide.

"So at 2 a.m., without telling anybody, I drove to the nearest 7–11 and looked for a pill bottle that resembled a slide. When I returned, I chucked the pills into the toilet at Cherokee and peeled off the label and proceeded back into the studio saying, 'Look what I found!' Ronnie at first didn't seem too keen on the idea of using it as a slide instead of one of his regular slides, but then he held it in his hand and said, 'Yeah, I think this might work.' And Geoff Workman, the engineer, said from behind the console, 'Good one, Ernie.' So we went to work in Studio B and Ronnie laid down his lead slide."

He was never credited on the *Gene Simmons* LP.

"The following week," Selgado continues, "it was the Cars at Cherokee, and if we would have stayed there any longer who knows how many more albums Ronnie would have played on!"

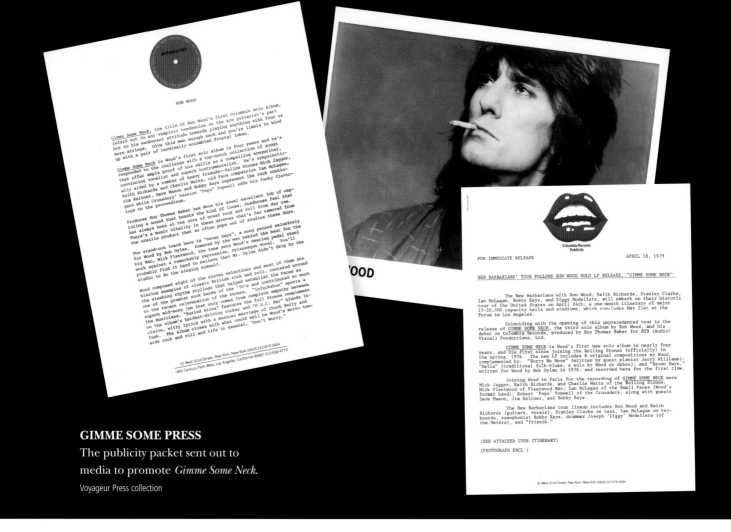

GIMME SOME PRESS

The publicity packet sent out to
media to promote *Gimme Some Neck*.

"I love Bob but whenever it was time to play, we'd have to drag him out of the bushes and start all over again. He was writing a song at the time called 'Seven Days,' and I know he liked me because, out of the blue, he just gave it to me. He said, 'You can have this one, Woody.'"

"Seven Days" was likely a castoff from Dylan's *Desire* sessions. He cut takes of it several times: There are rumors of unissued versions from the Columbia Studios in New York City in '75 and he may have tried again at Shangri-La during the Clapton sessions; a live version of the song from 1976 was eventually released on Dylan's *The Bootleg Series Volumes 1–3 (Rare & Unreleased) 1961–1991*. The song was a far cry from the epic symbolist-cum-beat poetry of *Desire*, and it's easy to see why Dylan left it off that album, or even the subsequent *Street Legal*. Instead, the lyrics stepped back to blues imagery; it was deceptively simple, desperately haunted.

Ronnie set "Seven Days" to a stinging blues riff, then sang the song in a voice that was more Dylan than Dylan—a raspy, nasal snarl. Critic Robert Christgau didn't cotton to Woody's singing, though,

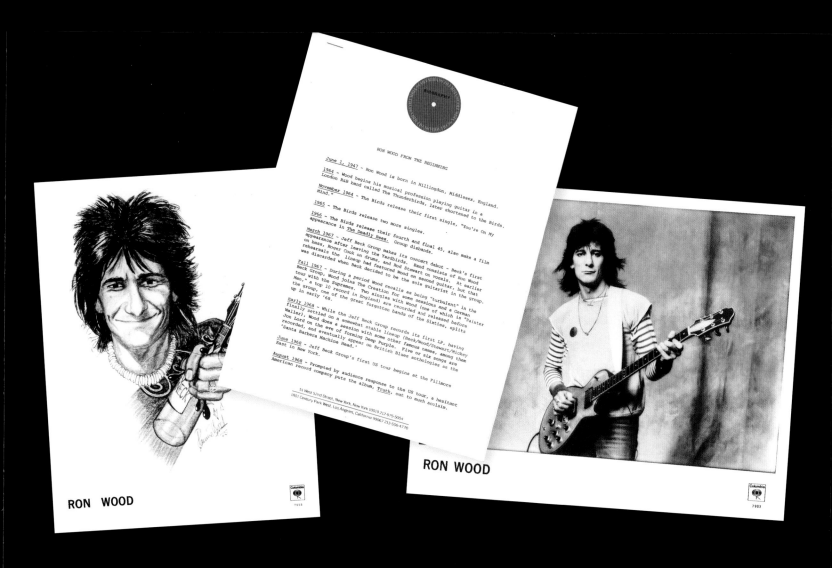

RON WOOD

RON WOOD

writing "this is a man who should never sing two songs in a row." This about a guy who had backed Rod Stewart and was covering Dylan! Ronnie may not have caused Pavarotti concern with his vocal range and emotional spectrum, but with his whiskey-toned voice and erotically charged delivery, he certainly got his message across at gut level. As Ronnie joked with *Creem*, "I had Jagger's full support. He gave me gargling lessons."

Regardless, "Seven Days" was a tour de force. Even Nick Kent hailed it: "What matters is that—with Wood sounding so uncannily like Dylan that you could fool even the most rabid Dylanophile at first play—the song is given a treatment that probably grants us the nearest approximation of how it would sound if Dylan and the Stones were to join forces on record."

And, if you add in an ample touch of the Faces, that is probably what made *Gimme Some Neck* sell so well.

Wood's previous solo albums—1974's *I've Got My Own Album to Do,* 1975's *Now Look,* and 1976's film soundtrack with Ronnie Lane, *Mahoney's Last Stand*—never racked up the sales, despite

"GIMME SOME NECK, THE TITLE OF RON WOOD'S FIRST COLUMBIA SOLO ALBUM, REFERS NOT TO ANY VAMPIRIC TENDENCIES ON THE ACE GUITARIST'S PART BUT TO HIS EXUBERANT ATTITUDE TOWARDS PLAYING ANYTHING WITH FOUR OR MORE STRINGS. GIVE THIS MAN ENOUGH NECK AND YOU'RE LIABLE TO WIND UP WITH A PAIR OF TERMINALLY SCRAMBLED FRONTAL LOBES."

**— COLUMBIA RECORDS
PRESS RELEASE**

some stellar songs, such as his masterpiece ballad "Mystifies Me." But *Gimme Some Neck* instantly became Wood's best-selling release, reaching No. 45 on the *Billboard* 200 during a 13-week run.

Columbia Records was thrilled. A CBS Memorandum on 8 December 1978 recapped a planning meeting with Ronnie, his manager Jason Cooper, and others: "The timing for this album could not be better. The Rolling Stones are hotter than they've ever been. With 'Some Girls' beginning to peak, Ron's album should pick up the excitement where the Stones left off." Another publicity department memo from 9 March 1979 stated, "With the release of *Gimme Some Neck*, Ron is now ready to be propelled into superstardom as a solo artist . . . . Gimmicks and over hype are not necessary for an artist such as Ron Wood."

That success set the scene: With a hot album out, time on his hands, Keith's debt to society to pay, and friends at the ready, why not hit the road?

CBS MEMORANDUM

RECEIVED
DEC 11 1978
SHELLY SELOVER

FROM: Ron Oberman
TO: SEE BELOW
DATE: December 8, 1978

Following is a recap of a meeting held Thursday, December 7, regarding Ron Wood. In attendance were Jason Cooper, Jack Craigo, Joe Mansfield, Ron Oberman and Mike Dilbeck.

1. Target date for album release is about February 15.

2. The timing for this album could not be better. The Rolling Stones are hotter than they've ever been. With "Some Girls" beginning to peak, Ron's album should pick up the excitement where the Stones left off.

3. This is a rock and roll album. Among the players are Mick Jagger, Dave Mason, Keith Richard, Charlie Watts, Mick Fleetwood and Ian McLaglen.

4. Pre-release of the album will be set up with a promo film featuring about three songs. The film should be completed by about January 21, approximately three weeks prior to release. This means that filming should commence the first week of January. Oberman and Levine should discuss.

5. Simultaneous with release of album, Ron Wood should embark on a promo tour of a number of cities. Sherwood should coordinate, as well as look into possibility of using corporate plane. Ron should meet one-on-one with radio programmers and DJ's.

   a. If company plane is obtained, we should consider flying along some music writers to create press excitement.

6. In mid-March, about four weeks after release, Jason is planning to put together a major 10-city performance tour featuring Ron Wood and an all-star band, hopefully including Keith Richard, Charlie Watts, Neil Young and others. (This information should be kept internal, as nothing is firm at this point.)

   a. Fred Humphrey should contact Jason and suggest which markets he feels will have the most impact for such a tour.

**Columbia Records
Publicity**

To Jason Cooper   March 9,1979
From Shelley Selover

RE: RON WOOD PRESS CAMPAIGN

There is no question that Ron Wood is a superstar in his own right. He made his mark with Rod Stewart and Faces and is an integral force of the world renowned Rolling Stones. His presence has added energy and vitality to every group he has worked with. And now, with the release of his debut Columbia album, Gimme Some Neck, Ron is now ready to be propelled into superstardom as a solo artist.

Our press campaign is basically three pronged: Album reviews concert reviews and selected interviews. Each will be carefully orchestrated to develop Wood's image as a solo artist. Our main objective is to use Wood's time sparingly. By adhering to this proposed plan we will achieve maximum quality publicity coverage on a caliber equal to Wood's position in our industry.

Gimmicks and over hype are not necessary for an artist such as Ron Wood. He is a viable, notable musician that only needs to make himself accessable to select press in order to create the kind of buzz we want.

Ron is a press worthy artist, and the Barbarian tour will only serve to sweeten the pot just that much more.

Timing is of the utmost importance to this campaign. The release of Gimme Some Neck is NEWS. The Barbarian tour is NEWS. And this is one of our strongest selling points. What we want to do is create a publicity whirlwind, an air of excitement. This is an event!!!!

Publicity press plans are as follows:

National Press

The key to maximum press coverate in the national publications is an

CHAPTER 3
HONEST RON'S ROCK, ROLL, JAZZ, AND R&B BAND

"KNOW ANY CHUCK BERRY?"

— RONNIE WOOD

FIRST BARBARIANS

(Opposite) Ronnie Wood had established a precedent for the New Barbarians with the pickup band he assembled to promote *I've Got My Own Record to Do* for two shows on 13 and 14 July 1974 at the Gaumont State Cinema in Kilburn, London. Rod Stewart and Keith Richards were there to help Woody out.

David Warner Ellis/Redferns/Getty Images

onnie Wood might just be the nicest, most genuine bloke in the rock 'n' roll biz. Many folks called him Honest Ron: You'd happily buy a used car from him (but since he's a Stone, you just might not want your daughter dating him). Thirty-one years young at the time of Barbarians, he had that eternal Marlboro glued to his lips, hair styled by electric shock, knife-edged visage, and a mile-wide smile. Keith called him a "chameleon" in his autobiography—which might help explain how Ronnie survived and thrived in the Faces and Stones.

And Ronnie Wood may just be the Henry Kissinger of rock 'n' roll: Who else could instantly and consistently put together such all-star "pickup bands," as he casually calls them, for studio sessions or tours the way he does.

MAC

Ronnie's Faces mate Ian McLagan signed on with the Barbarians to play keyboards. During the tour, he often hung out with assistant tour manager Robert "Mickey" Heyes, who had also worked with the Faces. The two of them "collected" jokes, as tour manager Richard Fernandez remembers, and would spend hours cracking each other up with their own special brand of humor and "hellacious" laughter. Bruce Silberman

In Ronnie's mind, a tour was essentially a party on wheels, and everyone wanted on the bus. As a Rolling Stone, he knew everyone, and those he didn't know, knew him. So putting together a band to join him in promoting *Gimme Some Neck* was just a matter of a few phone calls.

There was precedence, of course: the retroactively named First Barbarians. After cutting his first solo shot, 1974's *I've Got My Own Record to Do*, Woody assembled a band and played the songs live. Ronnie remembers: "When I made my first album in 1974 at Wick Studios in Richmond [his home studio], there was never any time to lose and this record was made (quickly) by many of my extremely talented friends. We took the songs from the record straight onto stage. Thus the First Barbarians were born." For backing, he rounded up some pals, listed for the show at the Gaumont State Theatre in Kilburn as simply "Woody and Friends." Those friends included Ian McLagan on keyboards and Keith Richards on guitar and backing vocals. The bottom end came courtesy of bassist Willie Weeks and drummer Andy Newmark, stalwart session cats who had played on many a great album: Weeks was part of American soul crooner Donny Hathaway's crew alongside guitarman Cornell Dupree, while Newmark drummed on Sly and the Family Stone's last great hurrah, 1973's *Fresh*; together, they had formed the rhythm section on George Harrison's *Dark Horse* and Randy Newman's *Good Old Boys*. Oh yeah, and Rod Stewart showed up at the Kilburn gigs, too.

The First Barbarians played two shows over the weekend of 13 and 14 July 1974. It was rough, it was rocking, and it was great, rowdy fun. Ronnie and Keith played together like they were Siamese twins, presaging Woody's '75 debut as a Stone. But at the time, the Kilburn show was more Faces than Stones: shambling rhythms, boozy bonhomie, and lots of grins—all highlighted by Stewart joyfully singing on Ronnie's "Mystifies Me" and "If You Gotta Make A Fool Of Somebody," and shaking a tambourine like nobody's business on "Take A Look At The Guy." The First Barbarians were good music, good friends, and good times—and proved for all time and without a shadow of a doubt (with all due apologies to Mae West, Marilyn, and Elton John) that no one looked finer in feathered finery than Ronnie Wood.

So, when Ronnie now looked at touring behind *Gimme Some Neck*, his fellow Stones guitarman, Keith Richards, was the first old friend he talked with. It would be a Rolling Stones–sized tour of America minus the rest of the Rolling Stones.

Keith was keen to move. He was on the run from heroin, Anita Pallenberg, and endless psychotherapy sessions. Given his torn and

frayed life, it may have been hard to fathom, but he was ready to turn over that proverbial new leaf. Ron Wood might have been low on the list of poster boys for AA, but paradoxically—and probably surprising no one more than himself—he aided and abetted Keith's recovery by providing the perfect venue for Keith to revive himself.

Keith headed west to the City of Angels where Ronnie was living. There, he fell in with Gary Schultz, one of Billy Preston's crew from the El Mocambo gigs. Schultz remembers the days: "In order to stay away from the people who were helping him get in trouble—including, unfortunately, his common-law wife Anita, because she was still doing things that were not good for *him* because the authorities were watching him and making sure he was staying clean—he came out to Los Angeles. And I had a rental station wagon and would drive him around every day and we became good friends."

Keith was feeling better than he had in years. Speaking of ending his years of heroin addiction with *Melody Maker*'s Chris Welch, he said, "I just got bored of it." Do you feel healthier? "Different. I suppose you could say healthier, although I must say, in all fairness to the poppy, that never once did I have a cold. I'm gonna blurt it out now, right? The cure to the common cold is there." He was now keeping his demons at bay with piratical draughts of various grogs.

"Mick didn't want to tour in 1979, but I did," Keith wrote in his autobiography. "I was put out and frustrated."

Schultz again: "Having been in trouble with the law and everything, going out on the road was Keith's safe place. Keith Richards is more himself when he's on the road and in front of an audience than when he's doing anything else."

Initially, though, Richards felt trepidation about the Barbarians. "When Ronnie decided to do the tour, he originally talked to a variety of people about joining in," Schultz remembers. "Neil Young

"MICK DIDN'T WANT TO TOUR IN 1979, BUT I DID. I WAS PUT OUT AND FRUSTRATED."

— KEITH RICHARDS

BOBBY KEYS

(Opposite) One of the prides of Lubbock, Texas—along with Buddy Holly, whom he played with—Keys had played on many a Stones recording and tour—and been booted off several as well. Henry Diltz

"KEITH RICHARDS IS MORE HIMSELF WHEN HE'S ON THE ROAD AND IN FRONT OF AN AUDIENCE THAN WHEN HE'S DOING ANYTHING ELSE."

— GARY SCHULTZ

wanted to do it, as well as a couple of other people. Keith said, 'If I'm going to do it, you're going to be the other guitar player—it's just going to be me and you.'

"Keith was very unsure of the whole thing from the get-go because this was the first time he had ever toured outside the Rolling Stones and he was putting his reputation on the line. He was concerned about making sure the tour was a success musically—he wasn't worried about the money."

Woody next talked to his old Faces mate and fellow First Barbarian Ian McLagan. From his natty shoes to his Beatles-esque mop, ex-mod Mac was always on board for a good time. He was fresh off the *Some Girls* sessions and tour, as well as overdubbing his keys on *Gimme Some Neck*. Mac remembered the pickup band fondly in his 1998 autobiography, *All the Rage*: "Nothing changes with Woody. By the time the album was ready to be released, he and Keith were looking for an excuse to play 'live' but as there was no Stones' tour in the offing, they put a touring band together for fun, and profit." The emphasis would be on the former.

Ronnie then asked Bobby Keys to bring his golden saxophone along for the ride. Hailing from the great state of Texas, Keys had a long and suitably sordid résumé with the Stones—and with rock 'n' roll in general. He began his career as a professional musician at the ripe young age of 15, touring with fellow Texan Buddy Holly as well as Bobby Vee. Keys first crossed paths with the Stones at the 1964 San Antonio Teen Fair, later signing on in '70 to tour with the band. That same year, Keys played on Eric Clapton's solo debut, George Harrison's multi-platter masterpiece *All Things Must Pass*, and was a cornerstone of Leon Russell's stellar band backing Joe Cocker on the Mad Dogs & Englishmen Tour. In 1969, Keys and Mick Taylor debuted on record with the Stones on the *Let It Bleed* track "Live With Me," and in '70 Keys added the raucous, lascivious sax solo to "Brown Sugar" that let you know exactly what you shoulda heard just around midnight.

THE METERS
(Opposite) Joseph "Zigaboo" Modeliste was the propulsion behind New Orleans' finest. Formed in 1965, the early lineup included (from front to back) vocalist and percussionist Cyril Neville (who joined in 1970), bassist George Porter Jr., vocalist and keyboardist Art Neville, guitarist Leo Nocentelli, and Ziggy on drums.
Voyageur Press collection

Keys served as best man at Jagger's wedding to Bianca Perez Morena de Macias—where Ronnie first met him in a bathroom in the south of France, replete with some substances that shouldn't be mentioned. Keys also became nearly inseparable from Keith. Alongside trumpeter Jim Price, Keys added his sax to the '71 and '72 tours, and was key to the '73 European tour's horn section—before he got thrown out of the band for being a bad influence. Legend has it that he filled a bathtub with Dom Perignon, then bathed in the champagne with a lady friend, to Jagger's ire. Since then, Keys made guest appearances at a handful of shows on the '75 and '78 U.S. tours, but had been left off albums since 1973's *Goats Head Soup* and hadn't been invited to the *Some Girls* sessions.

Despite Stones politics, Ronnie held no grudge with Keys. In fact, he had borrowed him from the Stones when they were recording next door to the Faces at Olympic Studios and Keys had tooted his horn on "Had Me A Real Good Time." They then proceeded to have a real good time indeed at Ronnie's Wick mansion. Their friendship continued through the years—and through, as Ronnie put it in his autobiography, "a very long journey together through freebase, coke, heroin, booze, more freebase and finally sobriety."

With the frontline in place, Ronnie looked to the bottom end. He asked Charlie Watts to revive his drumming role from the LP. At first Watts was in, but then he got busy with his Rocket 88 boogie-woogie band. Watts in turn recommended a fellow drummer that he had great respect for—Joseph "Zigaboo" Modeliste.

Ziggy had been the propulsion for the Meters, the band that practically defined New Orleans R&B. The group featured the crème de la crème of the Crescent City: At its launch in 1965, the Meters included frontman vocalist and keyboardist Art Neville, guitarman Leo Nocentelli, bassman George Porter Jr., and his cousin, Ziggy, on drums; they were soon filled out by vocalist and percussionist Cyril Neville. Their sound was pure tight. They combined melodic grooves with super-syncopated New Orleans "second-line" rhythms, layered on top with funkified guitar licks and punchy keyboard riffs. The Meters made the charts in '69 with their R&B hits "Sophisticated Cissy" and "Cissy Strut," followed in '70 by "Look-Ka Py Py"—soul classics that were the cornerstones to the house of funk. And along the way the Meters became Allen Toussaint's backing band, as well as his studio session band for his Sansu label.

The Stones in the person of Mick Jagger first flipped over the Meters' second-line grooves when the Meters played a party thrown by Paul McCartney in 1975 for the release of his *Venus and Mars* album aboard the RMS *Queen Mary* in Long Beach harbor. Smitten,

Jagger invited the band to open for the Stones' Tour of the Americas that year, followed by the Tour of Europe '76.

All good things come to end, and after a decade of revolutionizing music, the Meters fell apart in '77 when the Neville brothers left the band. After the Meters' demise, Ziggy had no steady gig going, as he remembers: "I was freelancing around, floundering around playing with this and that one—nothing really important, just keeping my chops good and making recording sessions when I could pick something up. So this came in the nick of time."

For Ziggy, the Barbarians' rock 'n' roll was not an easy adjustment—even after years of playing much more sophisticated rhythms and grooves. "It was certainly a learning experience for me. I'd never actually played rock. I was just an R&B-type of drummer. It was a little over my head, I gotta admit. It's a big stage when you're playing with Keith Richards and Ronnie Wood."

RETURN TO FOREVER
Chick Corea's band almost defined rock-jazz fusion, and included (from left) drummer Lenny White, bassist Stanley Clarke, Corea, and guitarist Al Di Meola. Voyageur Press collection

He says he made the switchover thanks largely to the influence of one man—his fellow on the bottom end, bassist Stanley Clarke.

Clarke became a bassist by accident. As a schoolboy in Philadelphia, he was late the day instruments were doled out in band class and a lonely acoustic bass was about all that was left. Graduating from the Philadelphia Musical Academy, he moved to New York City and began playing behind jazz greats Dexter Gordon, Horace Silver, Art Blakey, Dave Brubeck, Stan Getz, and others. In 1972, he joined Chick Corea's jazz-fusion ensemble Return to Forever, and over the next five years became one of the most influential bassists around, alongside Jaco Pastorius. At the same time, Clarke began releasing solo albums, including his stellar *School Days* in 1976. Return to Forever ended its run in '77, and Clarke was in Miami Beach on vacation when Ronnie called him about the Barbarians. Ron had met Stanley a couple years previously at the London bar Tramps, where Stanley complimented Ronnie on his bass playing on Jeff Beck's *Truth*—a compliment, indeed.

Now, when discussing the Barbarians, Woody's first question was, "Know any Chuck Berry?" It was a fair question coming from a rocker to a jazzer.

Clarke laughed, and replied, "Yeah, I know Chuck Berry songs." In fact, Stanley had *played* with Chuck: He backed him on *Dick Clark's Live Wednesday* TV show in '78.

"I've been called a jazz bass player, a funk bass player, a fusion bass player—they're just terms." Stanley says. "Just being a bass player, I always kept myself in a position to play anything that I heard and liked—a lot of different kinds of music from Bill Haley, Little Richard, and rockabilly; Count Basie, Miles Davis. I heard all kinds of things and was able to deliver on all those things so playing with these guys was not a stretch for me.

"A lot of that stuff, it's just language, like speaking French or Italian, and it's *understanding* the language. I've always been good with different musical languages because I was one of those kids who listened to everything, I didn't put one thing higher than the other."

Learning curve, jazz, whatever—Ronnie had faith in his new bottom end: "I knew they would adapt naturally—and put a new slant on their approach."

Last but hardly least, supporting the band was a tried-and-true crew with experience largely gained from working with the Faces. Richard Fernandez was the tour manager, a role he had held with the Faces and the Eagles. Ex-Face man Robert "Mickey" Heyes was Fernandez's assistant. Ken Graham was the lighting and stage designer as well as production manager. Buford T. Jones ran sound. Gary Schultz—who had worked with Billy Preston and the Stones— wore many a hat, from drum tech for Ziggy to Keith's confidant. Royden "Chuch" Magee was the guitar tech and Ronnie's all-around No. 1 man. Johnny Starbuck helped out onstage. Dave Reynolds was on loan from the Eagles. Ernie Selgado and Gary Kupski—or "Squinty," as Keith called him—helped out in the recording studio and with rehearsals. Security came thanks to the muscles of Big Jim Callahan—better known simply as J.C.—and Bob Bender. Henry Diltz was hired as official photographer.

Each crew member had their role, although as Schultz explains, "Any of us were interchangeable with each other; we were able to cover any problem on stage regardless of which musician was having the problem."

"IT WAS CERTAINLY A LEARNING EXPERIENCE FOR ME. I'D NEVER ACTUALLY PLAYED ROCK. I WAS JUST AN R&B-TYPE OF DRUMMER. . . . IT WAS A LITTLE OVER MY HEAD, I GOTTA ADMIT."

— ZIGGY MODELISTE

And they could do more than that. Ronnie's then girlfriend and future wife, Jo Howard, remembered in her autobiography, "Chuch had a team of roadies who prided themselves on being able to stay up all night, take drugs and still do their jobs the next day." Starbuck, Chuch, Schultz, and Salgado called their gang Hard Corps—"as in Marine Corps," Starbuck says—and the pun with "hardcore" was purely intentional.

There were also rumors of other Barbarians that would be joining the group onstage. Truth lurked behind some of those rumors; nothing but hot air inflated others.

Neil Young had expressed interest in joining Woody's band. He traveled down from San Francisco during band rehearsals to meet Keith for the first time. Ronnie told *Trouser Press*, "It wasn't really my idea to have him, but he kept on coming on so strong about it, saying, 'Don't forget, if Woody does a tour you can count me in. I'll do it for nothing. I just want to tour with him and Keith, a couple of English rock 'n' rollers.'"

The two chatted about possibilities, then Fernandez met officially with Young's manager, Elliot Roberts. Originally Elliot Rabinowitz, he was one of the most powerful—and eccentric—music managers on the California scene. Starting work at the prestigious, long-established William Morris Agency, he and David Geffen jumped ship to jumpstart their own modern firm for the new era of rock 'n' roll, Lookout Management. Roberts was at Geffen's side when he launched Asylum Records in 1971, and during the ensuing years worked with everyone from Joni Mitchell to Crosby, Stills, Nash & Young and Dylan to Linda Ronstadt and the Eagles. Fernandez remembers: "I went to Elliot Roberts' office, whom I knew pretty good, with Ronnie and Keith and they had discussions about it and I remember that it was positive that Neil wanted to do it."

The timing didn't synch, however. Young had a new child, was editing his *Rust Never Sleeps* film, then took a vacation to Acapulco;

soon word came back that Neil wasn't going to make the gig. McLagan says, "Neil got tired of sitting around waiting for them to get it organized, so he bailed out."

Still, Young's legacy remained with the band: He christened them with their name. *You guys are nothing but a bunch of Barbarians,* band members and crew remember Young saying. And so the name was set. Or at least, sort of. Someone discovered that there was already a band called the Barbarians: They hailed from Boston and played raucous garage rock in the mid-'60s. The name was duly and suitably revised to the *New* Barbarians.

McLagan also remembers Boz Scaggs coming to play during rehearsals: "Boz Scaggs came and sat in for a day, which was fun, but he didn't hang around either."

HARD CORPS
The Barbarians' crew included (from left) Gary Schultz, Royden "Chuch" Magee, and Johnny Starbuck. Along with Ernest Salgado, another crew member, they called themselves the Hard Corps—the pun with "hardcore" being intentional. Josephine Howard—Ronnie's girlfriend and future wife—was an honorary member, according to Starbuck.

Ringo Starr showed up as well. In fact, he drummed on a promotional film for *Gimme Some Neck* in April, playing "Seven Days" and "Buried Alive" with Ronnie, Mac, Bobby, and bassist Pops Powell. But Starr's schedule was full, and that one session was it.

Ronnie had earlier spoken to Jeff Beck in London about the Barbarians, and Beck said he'd love to join them, Ronnie told *Trouser Press.* Beck's manager, though, reported he was already committed, and that was that. Much the same thing occurred with Jimmy Page, who was also ready to sling his guitar with Ronnie, but then backed out.

Other names were also bandied about in the press. *Rolling Stone* writer Mikal Gilmore aired the rumors in print for all the rock 'n' roll world to read: "Wood—who's never led his own tour before and doesn't seem overly enthralled with the idea of being alone in the spotlight—has also invited Neil Young, Bob Dylan, Jeff Beck, David Bowie, Jimmy Page, Mick Jagger and Rod Stewart (who has his own tour to do) to appear separately or jointly at several of the shows. Suddenly, the post-Woodstock fantasy about the leading rock stars all materializing on the same stage seems like it may become a reality. In fact, only Jeff Beck has flatly refused to play."

As Ronnie told Gilmore in all innocent honesty: "I think even Mick. . . . is considering joining us for as many gigs as possible."

Gilmore then added, "Of course, whether any of the others actually turn up is another matter."

Where these rumors originated, no one seems to remember. Initially, Ronnie had indeed hoped to bring more "friends" into the band, as discussed at that CBS/Columbia Records powwow on 7 December 1978. But that idea changed once Keith and others were already aboard, as he told *Trouser Press* once the tour was underway: "I was real worried [about how well the shows would sell]. That's why I was possessed with getting another rock luminary on the tour. Now the group's attitude is the opposite, it'd be a drag if we do get anyone else. I want to quell the expectation of anyone but the New Barbarians."

"I KNEW THEY WOULD ADAPT NATURALLY— AND PUT A NEW SLANT ON THEIR APPROACH."

— RONNIE WOOD

Still the rumors persisted—they were too good not to. Several people pointed their finger at Ronnie's manager, Jason Cooper, for continuing to spread the word about surprise guests at the shows, perhaps out of fear that Wood and Co. weren't enough of a draw. Or that the draw could simply be made larger.

Whatever the source, the rumors of other Barbarians would plague the tour until the band's finale.

CHAPTER 4
NEOPHYTE BARBARIANS

"I WANT TO SEE BLOOD."

— RONNIE WOOD

BARBARIANS REHEARSALS, APRIL 1979
(Opposite) The Barbarians started rehearsing in the
spring of 1979 at MGM's Culver Studios in Culver City,
California. Here, they had the space to set up a replica of
the entire tour stage. Alan Pariser/Geoff Gans collection

**SATURDAY NIGHT LIVE
REHEARSALS**
The friendship established between
the Stones and *SNL* cast members
led to their meeting up during the
Barbarians' rehearsals in April '79 in
Culver City. Ken Regan/Camera 5/Contour by
Getty Images

The shenanigans began right from the start, even before the band hit the road. And in retrospect, that seems only proper and right.

To learn Ronnie's songs, lock in the bottom end, and hone their chops, the proto-Barbarians convened in the spring of 1979 for two weeks of rehearsals at a soundstage at MGM's Culver Studios in Culver City, California. Here, they had the elbow room to set up a replica of the entire tour stage and get down to practicing. Almost as soon as they counted in the first song, though, things began to get out of hand.

The Stones had made a guest appearance on *Saturday Night Live*—then the hottest TV show going—on 7 October 1978 to pimp their new *Some Girls* LP, playing "Beast Of Burden," "Respectable," and "Shattered," as well as a *Tomorrow Show* parody between Dan Aykroyd and Jagger, plus an Olympia Café skit with Woody and Watts. Not only was the show a hit, but Aykroyd and John Belushi —Stones fans, natch—became buddies with the band. The *SNL* duo of Belushi and Aykroyd had launched their side careers as the Blues

"JOHN BELUSHI AND OTHERS FROM *SATURDAY NIGHT LIVE* WERE IN TOWN REHEARSING A BLUES BROTHERS THING AND THEY DROPPED BY REHEARSALS. . . . SO THERE WAS A LOT OF YAKKING AND PLAYING AROUND."

— RICHARD FERNANDEZ

Brothers playing Slim Harpo's "I'm A King Bee" for a sketch on the 17 January 1976 episode. Now, the Brothers had a chance to play the blues for real.

"John Belushi and others from *Saturday Night Live* were in town rehearsing a Blues Brothers thing and they dropped by rehearsals. I knew Woody and Keith were old friends with Belushi, so there was a lot of yakking and playing around," says tour manager Fernandez. The pals and other hangers-on soon dominated the rehearsals, though. Schultz explains: "John Belushi had an ear infection, so he couldn't fly back to New York because of the pressure while on the plane. Everyone loved Belushi, but he was a hard guy to get rid of. John always wanted to be part of whatever was happening. One evening, John was doing his James Brown routine. Josephine [Howard] was standing on a ladder shining a flashlight on him, Chevy Chase was playing piano, Aykroyd was playing drums, and John was singing all these James Brown songs.

"Belushi was staying at the Playboy Mansion and couldn't get back to New York to be on *Saturday Night Live*, so they filmed an

**BARBARIANS REHEARSAL,
APRIL 1979**
(Above) Stanley Clarke adapts
to the rock 'n' roll culture of the
Barbarians. Alan Pariser/Geoff Gans collection

BARBARIANS ART
(Opposite) At the same time as he
was rehearsing his band, Ronnie
was also designing the stage (with
Ken Graham's help) and creating
this artwork that would appear on
Barbarians tour posters, T-shirts,
passes, and more. Gary Greenberg collection

announcement and they show him laying in a hospital bed. John
says he's there on doctor's order because he can't fly due to the
ear infection, but he promises to be back next week. And as he's
explaining this, these Playboy bunnies dressed like nurses—*half*-
dressed like nurses—are crawling into bed with him, and John's got
that Belushi smile.

"It was fun and everything but the band couldn't get nothing
done. Keith took me aside and said, 'Hey, get rid of Belushi. Take him
wherever he wants to go, do whatever he wants to do. We're trying
to get the rehearsals done.'"

As the scene at the Culver City rehearsal space spun out of control, Wood's crew booked time at the Beach Boys' Brothers Recording
Studio in Santa Monica (renamed after being sold in '78 as Crimson
Sound), where they could escape and focus. So they ultimately had
two rehearsals space that they used simultaneously.

"THE BAND COULDN'T GET NOTHING DONE. KEITH TOOK ME ASIDE AND SAID, 'HEY, GET RID OF BELUSHI. TAKE HIM WHEREVER HE WANTS TO GO, DO WHATEVER HE WANTS TO DO. WE'RE TRYING TO GET THE REHEARSALS DONE.'"

— GARY SCHULTZ

"When Keith and Woody decided it was time to get down to business, it was, 'OK, we're focused.' And the other guys, they were pros, so when it was time to play, they were like *boom*, 'Let's go!'" Fernandez says. "The band was very focused on rehearsing. They really wanted to get a good product out there. All the musicians that Ronnie had chosen to come and play were very respectful of each other and what they did, and everybody wanted to do it good for Ronnie."

Gary Schultz remembers the rehearsals running from 10 p.m. to 6 a.m., night after night. Mac explained the method to their madness: "Hours after the arranged start time, we'd arrive, chat, do a couple of lines, laugh, play, smoke a joint, sip a drink, do another line, play another song until Keith had had enough or we'd run out of blow."

For Stanley Clarke, this meant around-the-clock workshifts, as Ronnie remembered: "Stanley was in the middle of mixing his new double LP [1979's *I Wanna Play for You*] so he'd be starting in the studio at midday, going through to midnight, then coming down and rehearsing 'til 5 a.m. He was a real trooper."

The Barbarians had just two weeks to get it together: They were booked for their debut shows on 22 April in Oshawa, Canada. And they needed the practice—or at least Ziggy says *he* did.

"I was learning a whole 'nother genre of songs and the specific parts that *made* the songs, and I had to really try to do the best I could to give them what they needed," he remembers. "To me, I loved the *feel* of rock and roll, so that was right up my alley, but it was a big learning curve because I had to learn how to listen in a different way."

Usually, a band is built from the bottom end: The drummer and bass player lock in together to create the foundation for the music. That's what Ziggy was aiming for, and he credits Stanley Clarke with working the magic to make it happen.

BARBARIANS REHEARSALS, APRIL 1979
(Opposite) Ronnie Wood soaks up the sounds of his new band. Alan Pariser/ Geoff Gans collection

"LET ME SAY THIS: STANLEY CLARKE HAS BEEN TOUCHED BY GOD. AND LET ME SAY THIS: I DON'T CARE HOW MANY BASS PLAYERS YOU PUT OUT THERE, THERE WOULD NEVER, EVER BE ANOTHER STANLEY CLARKE."

— ZIGGY MODELISTE

BARBARIANS REHEARSALS, APRIL 1979

Culver Studios not only allowed the band plenty of space to practice but also gave Ronnie, Keith, and production manager Ken Graham a life-size stage to work with as they designed the band's special "look."

Alan Pariser/Geoff Gans collection

BARBARIANS REHEARSALS, APRIL 1979
Ziggy gets comfortable behind his new drum kit, specially painted in Barbarians' blood-red for Ronnie. As he remembers, "When you have seven cats and three or four of them play together all the time but you got other people who are just making the whole scene and you're playing music that you've just been introduced to and you're learning what you can learn about it, it just takes time to really sink in, to really bite down into the apple." Alan Pariser/Geoff Gans collection

BARBARIANS REHEARSALS, APRIL 1979
(Opposite) Mac mans his multitude of keyboards. Alan Pariser/ Geoff Gans collection

"Let me say this: Stanley Clarke has been touched by God. And let me say this: I don't care how many bass players you put out there, there would never, ever be another Stanley Clarke. That cat is just nothing short of tremendous. He makes the drummer *shine*. He was very serious about his music, and I learned a lot from him just by his demeanor."

While Ronnie was fending off the Blues Brothers' antics, getting his band in sync, and overseeing tour plans, he was also central to designing how the Barbarians would *look* on stage. Whereas the Faces had a completely white stage setup, from the flooring to the amp grills, Woody envisioned something new.

"I want to see blood—a lot of blood, a lot of red—on stage," production manager Ken Graham remembers Ronnie saying. Forget painting it black; the whole stage was going to be red. Graham had a theatrical background and worked a lot of rock 'n' roll tours, but he had never quite had *that* request.

Graham's résumé included designing the lighting for the Eagles's tours, which pioneered the dramatic effects that became the norm for the biggest rock acts in later years. "I'm one of the dinosaurs who got

BARBARIANS REHEARSALS, APRIL 1979

The band quickly found its groove. Ziggy remembers that playing rock 'n' roll was a "big learning curve" for him, but Stanley Clarke says Ziggy was just being humble. Alan Pariser/Geoff Gans collection

the whole thing going," he says. But regardless of past stage-and-light design motifs, the Barbarians were going to have something new.

Ronnie envisioned that blood-red theme to tie in with the Barbarians' name, of course. And as an artist, he had distinct ideas about the scene, the mood, the *drama*, he wanted to create.

"The set was co-designed by Ronnie, Keith, and myself," Graham says. "We had two overnight sessions. I took notes, made some drawings, brought them back to Ronnie and Keith for review, and then away we went.

"We didn't want to see all the stagehands when the band was on stage, so we built a scrim wall to hide them. The wall and the floor were white, with rivers of blood that came down and flowed outward toward the audience with squiggles and trails."

Graham then designed the lighting to have follow spots and Super Troupers on the back of the stage just over the wall. The lights shot up over the musicians' heads, hitting a mirror that was hung just in front of the scoreboards in the arenas they'd play, and then the beam of light was brought back down onto the artists. Working with

Showco Inc. out of Dallas for lights and sound—the Stones' usual vendor at the time—Graham designed the lighting to be saturated with blue and red gels instead of the usual amber or white lights. He says, "This accentuated the bloody red stage. When Ronnie wanted it to go red, *it went red*." The lighting design was novel and graphic and thoroughly dramatic. "This was a very cool look," Graham says, "and Ronnie said he loved it."

The best was still to come.

"At the back of the stage in the center, we created a room with walls that were seven to eight feet high that the band could run back into to take a break during a drum solo or between songs," Graham explains. "And just to protect their privacy, we put a roof on the room so that people up in the seats couldn't see into the room and see anything that *might* be going on there."

The stage was set up at Culver Studios and stowed away time and again as the crew rehearsed their part of the proceedings. "It all had to fit into road cases and hampers, and I made it easyto put up and take down and foolproof along the way," Graham remembers.

BARBARIANS REHEARSALS, APRIL 1979
Keith takes a seat at the piano alongside Mac to sing "Apartment #9." After performing the song at the Largo, Maryland, show on 5 May 1979, Mac christened Keith "The Rebel Yell from London, England."
Alan Pariser/Geoff Gans collection

BARBARIANS REHEARSALS, APRIL 1979

Despite Keith's skepticism, the band's horn section was at times two-saxes strong, as Ronnie had recently taught himself to play. Alan Pariser/Geoff Gans collection

BARBARIANS REHEARSALS, APRIL 1979

(Opposite) Keith teaches Stanley the intricacies of Chuck Berry's duck walk. Alan Pariser/Geoff Gans collection

"AT THE BACK OF THE STAGE . . . WE CREATED A ROOM WITH WALLS . . . THAT THE BAND COULD RUN BACK INTO TO TAKE A BREAK DURING A DRUM SOLO OR BETWEEN SONGS. AND JUST TO PROTECT THEIR PRIVACY, WE PUT A ROOF ON THE ROOM SO THAT PEOPLE UP IN THE SEATS COULDN'T SEE INTO THE ROOM AND SEE ANYTHING THAT *MIGHT* BE GOING ON THERE."

— KEN GRAHAM

28 APRIL 1979

(Opposite and top) With the rehearsal period concluded, the shows begin; the Barbarians play the International Amphitheater in Chicago, Illinois. Paul Natkin/Getty Images

That blood-red theme carried over to the musicians' gear as well. The grill covers on the backline of amps were scarlet—a trick Ronnie had adopted and then adapted from the Faces, who once toured with an all-white stage. And even Ziggy's drum kit fit the theme.

"Ronnie Wood had a set of drums for me," Ziggy remembers. "And he's an artist supreme—cat comes up with these drawings and stuff, he's off the hook with that, don't know where he learned that, he's very good. So he came up with this idea and he says, 'Hey man, why don't you let me paint these drums and make all these designs on them.' So that's what he did. I think it was an old Rogers or Slingerland kit, and he painted them *red*."

With Schultz chaperoning Belushi out of the band's way, Fernandez finalizing concert venues across the country, Graham making good use of every can of red paint he could scrounge up, Stanley Clarke reacquainting himself with Chuck Berry's oeuvre, and Ziggy learning how to nail that rock 'n' roll backbeat, the Barbarians were coming together. As Ziggy remembers, "The only sad part about the whole thing was that we were just beginning to sit down at this table like the United Nations, trying to figure who and how we were going to fit into this equation musically. We only had so and so many days to rehearse and then *chooo*, we're right into it."

— CHAPTER 5 —
BLIND DATE

"GO NUTS!"

— JOHN BELUSHI

CANADIAN NATIONAL INSTITUTE FOR THE BLIND CONCERT, OSHAWA, 22 APRIL 1979
(Opposite) The Rolling Stones take the stage for their second show after the Barbarians opened the evening at the Oshawa Civic Auditorium, playing two benefit concerts following Keith Richards' drug bust.

Richard E. Aaron/Redferns/Getty Images

PLAYBOY AIRPORT

Mac, Ronnie, and Keith get ready to board the airplane taking them from the Playboy Club in Lake Geneva, Wisconsin, to the Oshawa show. Henry Diltz

The Barbarians' debut shows were Keith's "Get Out of Jail Free" cards: Two benefit concerts for the Canadian National Institute for the Blind, on 22 April 1979. Yet there were reservations on the band's part. There were first-show jitters, of course. These were combined with the fact that they'd be opening for none other than the Rolling Stones. But most of all, there were concerns about Keith setting foot again on Canadian soil and returning to the scene of the crime.

Tour manager Richard Fernandez organized the band's logistics around this anxiety. The musicians would stay in the United States, fly in for the two shows, then immediately jump back on their private jet and get the hell out of Dodge.

The Barbarians were booked into suites at the Playboy Club in Lake Geneva, Wisconsin, an idyllic resort town northwest of Chicago with its own private jet runway. This would serve as the band's headquarters, rehearsal space, and starting off point for further shows throughout the Midwest.

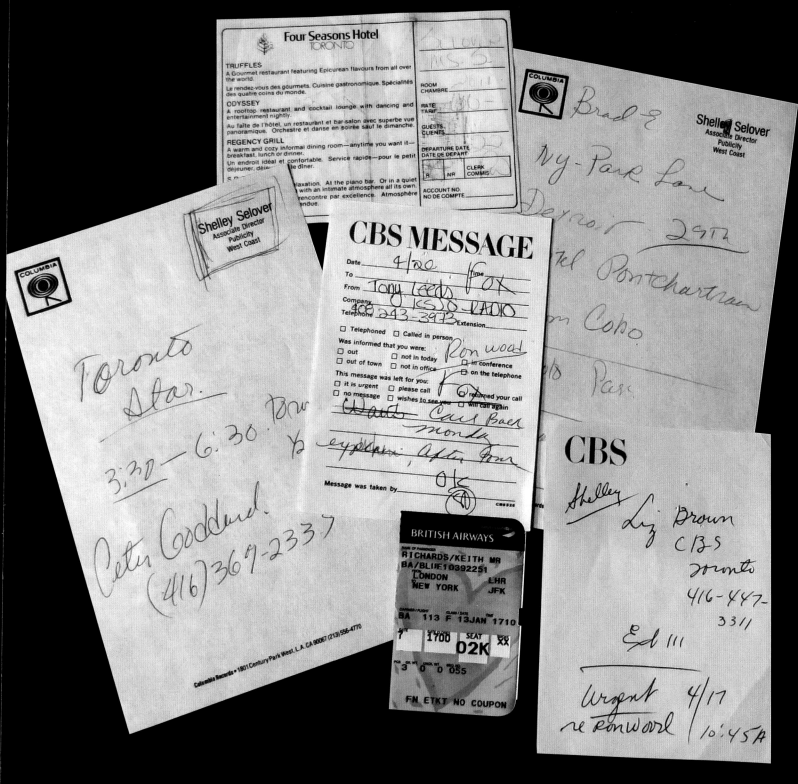

Miscellaneous memos, receipts, and
Keith Richards' boarding pass from the
days leading up to the Barbarians tour.
Gary Greenberg collection

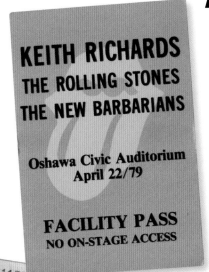

"TORONTO BOUND: PLEASE TAKE THE TIME TO ASSURE THAT YOU WILL BE CLEAN UPON ARRIVAL. SKIP THE SOAP AND GO RIGHT FOR THE VACUUM."

— NEW BARBARIANS ITINERARY

"Going to Canada, Keith's visa was a concern, so we just went in and out," Fernandez says. "I wasn't sure what could or couldn't happen to us when we got there, so we figured this would be the best way to get in, without any luggage, without any*thing*, you know—just people. Get in and get out, spic and span."

Or, as the official itinerary that was given to all Barbarians stated prominently in the top left corner: "Toronto bound: Please take the time to assure that you will be clean upon arrival. Skip the soap and go right for the vacuum."

Having one stationary HQ also served another purpose: It made tour planning a whole lot simpler—especially seeing as sugar-daddy Woody was paying for the 727. As Fernandez explains, "Being based out of the Playboy Club made everything easier, not needing to change hotels every other day."

Not to mention the cottontailed staff.

To maintain that proverbial spic and span, Woody and Keith also had their trusted bagman, Robert Heyes, known to one and all as Mickey. Fernandez: "Mickey was my righthand man, the assistant tour manager, and he worked with the Faces, the Eagles, and later with Tom Petty. He did the bags, the luggage, and carried a lot of 'things' that Ronnie and Keith didn't want to carry. He was always available to Keith and Woody at any time of the day or night, and that's the way Keith and Woody liked it. They trusted him—he was an extremely trustworthy person."

So, on 21 April, the Barbarians flew from Long Beach to Lake Geneva at 1 p.m. Comfortably settled into the Playboy Club, the

OSHAWA TICKET AND FACILITY PASS
(Top and middle) Gary Greenberg collection

OSHAWA STAGE PASS
(Bottom) Matt Lee collection

Barbarians rehearsed through the night before Keith's blind date. They then flew up to Toronto on the morning of the 22 April shows.

"The Customs in Toronto were really easy on us, as if none of us had any previous convictions. But there was nothing to worry about as Keith wasn't carrying any drugs," McLagan remembered in his autobiography. "When Mick, Charlie and Bill [Wyman] arrived from England, they picked on Bill of all people, and went through him like a dose of salts. They frisked the only person in the whole outfit who'd never taken a drug in his life."

From the airport, the Barbarians drove the 60 kilometers to the concert venue at the Oshawa Civic Auditorium.

The hall was the hallowed home of the Oshawa Generals hockey team, and so well used to its share of rough-and-tumble fun. Still, the gentle citizenry harbored the usual fears that their peaceful burg was about to be sacked and burned—especially in light of what had

STONES FANS
Among the crowd waiting for the first show at the Oshawa Civic Auditorium were Andy Salter, 93, and his wife Betsy, 80, who received free tickets from the Canadian National Institute for the Blind. The Canadian Press/UPC/Gail Harvey

> "WHEN MICK, CHARLIE AND BILL [WYMAN] ARRIVED FROM ENGLAND, THEY PICKED ON BILL OF ALL PEOPLE, AND WENT THROUGH HIM LIKE A DOSE OF SALTS. THEY FRISKED THE ONLY PERSON IN THE WHOLE OUTFIT WHO'D NEVER TAKEN A DRUG IN HIS LIFE."
>
> — IAN MCLAGAN

happened during the Stones' last, 1977 visit to Toronto. Groupies were already swarming the band's Four Seasons Hotel in Toronto; restless throngs of other fans now encircled the auditorium, waiting impatiently for the doors to be unlocked. As Johnny Starbuck remembers, "The population of that small town must have tripled those couple of days. There were people camped out in tents in the parks and even the highway medians. It just goes to show, that if you announce a small Stones show too far in advance, it gives every Stones nut in the world time to get there." But despite worries about having the Stones come to town, the local constabulary of 40 police officers handled the crowd of 10,000 for the two shows at 4:00 and 8:30 politely, peacefully, and efficiently. Reported Chet Flippo in *Rolling Stone*, "The only thing that burned was the music."

The Barbarians were welcomed onstage first by blind DJ Cliff Lorimer of CKDK Radio in Woodstock, Ontario. He then handed the

CANADIAN NATIONAL INSTITUTE FOR THE BLIND CONCERT, OSHAWA, 22 APRIL 1979

In keeping with the blood-red stage and lighting, Keith dressed himself all in red for the afternoon show—red T-shirt and red leather pants. Richard Aaron

CANADIAN NATIONAL INSTITUTE FOR THE BLIND CONCERT, OSHAWA, 22 APRIL 1979

(Opposite) Jagger and Richards onstage at Oshawa. Richard Aaron

**CANADIAN NATIONAL
INSTITUTE FOR THE BLIND
CONCERT, OSHAWA,
22 APRIL 1979**
Ronnie and Keith trade licks during
the Barbarians' evening show. The
New Barbarians' setlist included
"Sweet Little Rock & Roller," "F.U.C.
Her," "Breathe On Me," "Infekshun,"
"I Can Feel The Fire," "Am I Grooving
You," "Seven Days," and "Before They
Make Me Run."

mike off to an obviously amped-up John Belushi, who screamed out his introduction, which was similar at both afternoon and evening shows:

"Greetings from fellow Canadian Dan Aykroyd! I don't know if you know who I am: I work on a sleazy late-night TV show on Saturday and I did a movie and an album with Dan Aykroyd, fellow Canadian. He's in the Bahamas, the lazy bastard, and he told me to tell you to all go nuts tonight! Now, this band that's coming up, the opening act, they used to be called the New Vegetarians but they finished a steak and they're now called the New Barbarians. On drums, one of the greatest drummers in the world, Ziggy from the Meters! On keyboards, Ian McLagan. On bass, Stanley Clarke! On the sax, the legendary Bobby Keys! And now Keith Richards and Ron Wood, come on out here! The New Barbarians—go nuts!"

And with that, Ronnie kicked the Barbarians into first gear with "Breathe On Me," the introspective rocker from his 1975 solo LP *Now*

"THIS BAND THAT'S COMING UP, THE OPENING ACT, THEY USED TO BE CALLED THE NEW VEGETARIANS BUT THEY FINISHED A STEAK AND THEY'RE NOW CALLED THE NEW BARBARIANS."

— JOHN BELUSHI

Look. Not surprisingly, the Barbarians' sound was loose, tatterdemalion rock 'n' roll, but they quickly pulled themselves into a shambling groove. They segued into the mid-tempo "Come To Realise," before finally pulling out the stops on "Infekshun," Ziggy's drumming both anchoring and propelling them along as the Barbarians got their ya-ya's out. They rambled through "Lost And Lonely" and the 1967 Freddie Scott soul grind "Am I Grooving You" from Wood's *I've Got My Own Album to Do*, before hitting it hard on Dylan's "Seven Days." Keith next took center stage for his first-ever concert rendition of his *Some Girls* vocal contribution "Before They Make Me Run." And then the band was gone. It was a short and sweet set, but the show was far from over.

"As The New Barbarians . . . finished their first set at Civic Auditorium, the stage lights went down. Then a single white spotlight picked out Richards, his rooster hairdo aflop, sitting on a stool and holding an acoustic guitar. When he hit the first notes of 'Prodigal Son,' Mick Jagger materialized beside him from out of the backstage darkness, and a frightening roar—almost like halleluja—rose spontaneously from 5000 devotees," wrote Flippo in *Rolling Stone*. The rest of the Stones then joined them and the full band charged into Chuck Berry's "Let It Rock." After a songlist rife with *Some Girls* tunes, the Barbarians filled out the band for a finale as they all jammed on an eight-minute-long "Jumpin' Jack Flash." As Stanley remembers,

CANADIAN NATIONAL INSTITUTE FOR THE BLIND CONCERT, OSHAWA, 22 APRIL 1979
(Overleaf) For both their afternoon and evening shows, the Stones played sets packed with *Some Girls* tunes, along with Chuck Berry's "Let It Rock" and their own "Starfucker." Richard E. Aaron/ Redferns/Getty Images

"IT WAS ABSOLUTELY THE MOST ELECTRIFYING EXPERIENCE I'VE EVER HAD ON STAGE. JAGGER WAS TOTALLY PUMPED UP, 150 PERCENT ON ALL THE WAY!"

— STANLEY CLARKE

BARBARIAN FANS
(Top) John Belushi and Jo Howard watch the show from the sidelines.
Courtesy Gary Schultz

BREAKTIME
(Bottom) Gary Schultz and Ziggy take a needed rest against a wall painted in Barbarian artwork. Courtesy Gary Schultz

CANADIAN NATIONAL INSTITUTE FOR THE BLIND CONCERT, OSHAWA, 22 APRIL 1979
(Opposite) Richards wails on the '50s Stratocaster that he brought with him during the whole tour but rarely played on stage after Oshawa.
Richard Aaron

"It was absolutely the most electrifying experience I've ever had on stage. Jagger was totally pumped up, 150 percent on all the way!"

Leaving the stage without doing an encore, the Stones received a rousing five minutes of boos. But they had a whole other show still to go.

And they hadn't disappointed. As Flippo swooned, "It was obvious the Stones were alive and well and raising hell."

The backstage circus was alive and well, too. Belushi was center stage and enjoying every minute of it—as was the usual entourage of hangers-on, radio personalities, industry suits, and various other snakecharmers and smokesellers. And because it was a Canadian National Institute for the Blind benefit, there were seeing-eye dogs added to the pack. McLagan remembered the goings-on: "Poor Bill wasn't having a great day [after his customs shakedown at the airport]. Somebody bumped into him backstage, and without looking or thinking, he said, 'Why don't you watch where you're going, what are you, blind or something?' He was."

Of the 10,000 seats for the pair of shows, 2,600 tickets had been distributed free to blind fans; the take from the purchased tickets went to the CNIB. The Stones also printed a braille program for the shows, but it was never handed out, reportedly due to protests from an unspecified group for the blind that a braille program was patronizing. Jagger later laughed this off, saying, "That's like illiterate people complaining they're being discriminated against because a program has words on it and they can't read."

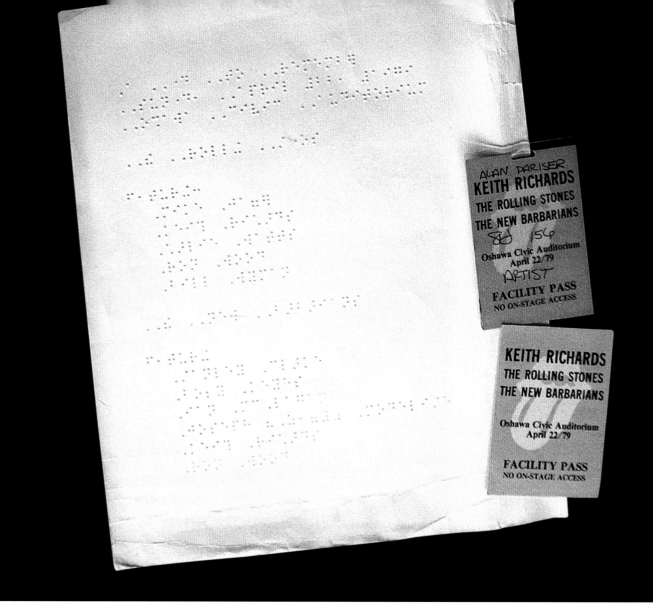

After a bit of R & R, the Barbarians were back, Ronnie's double-stop licks on his Zemaitis guitar jumpstarting the evening with Chuck Berry's "Sweet Little Rock & Roller." The band sounded tight and right this time around, going for blood on hard-rocking tunes including "F.U.C. Her" and *I've Got My Own Album to Do*'s kickoff cut, the reggae-sparked "I Can Feel The Fire," which Jagger had originally helped Woody with in trade for their collaboration on "It's Only Rock 'n Roll (But I Like It)."

Keith was obviously chuffed by the rock 'n' roll both the Barbarians and Stones were delivering. Noted Flippo, "Keith, now healthy and energetic after his cure from heroin addiction, had never played better—or cockier. He was all over the stage, confidently sweeping his right arm overhead with each run, goosing Jagger with his guitar neck." Toronto's *The Globe and Mail* newspaper summed things up with the headline: "Jumping Keith Richards shows old flash."

CANADIAN NATIONAL INSTITUTE FOR THE BLIND CONCERT, OSHAWA, 22 APRIL 1979
The infamous braille program for the CNIB shows that was never handed out due to protest that it was patronizing. François Fucqua collection

CANADIAN NATIONAL INSTITUTE FOR THE BLIND CONCERT, OSHAWA, 22 APRIL 1979
(Opposite) The encore for both Stones' sets was "Jumpin' Jack Flash" featuring the combined forces of the Stones and New Barbarians. Richard E. Aaron/Redferns/Getty Images

CANADIAN NATIONAL INSTITUTE FOR THE BLIND CONCERT, OSHAWA, 22 APRIL 1979
At the end of the day, the Barbarians hightailed it back to the Playboy Club. The guitarists had played four sets, and as tour manager Richard Fernandez puts it: "Ronnie and Keith worked their asses off that day." Richard E. Aaron/Redferns/Getty Images

The Stones replayed their afternoon show's set—during which four music-crazed fans scaled the rafters of the auditorium and danced away on twelve-inch-wide beams high above the heads of the rest of the audience. After another blistering "Jumpin' Jack Flash," both bands headed their own ways.

The Oshawa doubleheader would be the last live show the Stones played for two and a half years until the American tour 1981 behind *Tattoo You*.

"Ronnie and Keith worked their asses off that day," tour manager Richard Fernandez remembers. "They were the opening act, and then they played with the Stones—and they did two shows. They were beat at the end of that."

That night, while the rest of the Stones stayed over in Toronto, Keith was back at the Playboy Club with the cottontails, safely tucked in for the night. Or something like that.

Sentenced to play

Keith Richards of the Rolling Stones plays guitar during a benefit concert for the blind of Oshawa, Ontario, Can., near Toronto, Sunday night. Richards, who had been convicted of heroin possession, was ordered to play a benefit concert for the Canadian Nastional Institute for the Blind as part of his sentence.

AP Laserphoto

ROLLING STONES!

ENTERTAINMENT

Jumping Keith Richards shows old flash

Thugs steal fan's tickets

SENTENCED TO PLAY
(Top) Just as his Toronto bust had made headlines, Keith's benefit concert also made the news across North America. Curt Angeledes collection

BLIND ANGEL
(Middle) Rita Bédard on the day after the Oshawa shows, sporting an Oshawa '79 Stones button. Curt Angeledes

HAPPY
(Bottom left) A quick picture snapped through the limo window of a winking Keith Richards the day after the Oshawa show. Curt Angeledes

CHAPTER 6
STORMING THE GATES

"I WANTED TO DO THIS IN STYLE."

— RONNIE WOOD

CREW

New Barbarians

New Barbarians

Authorized

AJOR EVENTS
sents
BARBARIANS
★ ★ ★ ★ ★
ARENA
OF MICHIGAN
ANN ARBOR, MICHIGAN
TUESDAY
8:00 P.M.

PRICE
NO REFUND
NO EXCHANGE
$12.50
SEC 27 ROW 24 SEAT 6
GOLD TIER

DETROIT, 28 APRIL 1979
(Opposite) Keith and Stanley in the
spotlight. Robert Matheu

Inset Gary Greenberg collection

There was little time for sleep anyway. Following the Oshawa doubleheader, the Barbarians had one day to recover before the tour proper began. On 24 April, they boarded Ronnie's 727 and flew into Willow Run Airport in Ypsilanti, Michigan, on their way to headlining at the Crisler Arena in nearby Ann Arbor.

The Barbarians were still a work-in-progress. As *Washington Post* reporter Eve Zibart noted, the on-the-run, make-do character of the tour showed up in multiple little ways backstage. Several road cases and assorted equipment boxes bore the stencil "Small Faces"; a couple others read "The Eagles." Only a handful proudly bore a hasty "Ron Wood." And that blood-red stage was still getting infusions of Ronnie's desired redness: Last bits and pieces of the set were being spraypainted out in the back parking lot.

Onstage, Ken Graham and crew were making things happen by the skin of their teeth. Zibart wrote that the set looked "less like an enchanted forest than a Japanese B movie version of moon rock." The

ANN ARBOR, 24 APRIL 1979
Barbarian welcoming committee.
Robert Alford

spots and Super Troupers were being tested and retested, blazing brighter than the Second Coming. And all afternoon, while the sound was checked, adjusted, and rechecked, Ziggy's drum tech, Gary Schultz, beat on the bass drum, blow after deafening blow. In the midst of all this mayhem, two of the crew managed to find the peace and solace to take a 30-minute nap in folding chairs.

Meanwhile, back on the 727, champagne was on ice, ready and set for the after-show cork-popping on the flight home.

Finally, 45 minutes after their scheduled start time, the Barbarians hit the stage.

"The crowd is wired," the *Post* reported. "Frisbees swoop and soar, even after the lights go down. The volume reverberates under the ribs like a cardiac convulsion. . . . The omens are good."

Then, from the PA system, came the voice of God, or at least of Johnny Starbuck, who recalls: "Right before the first show, Richard Fernandez realized that one thing he had forgotten to do was assign someone to introduce the band. The band was all ready in the wings and the show was ready to begin but Richard didn't have anyone to make the announcement. There was a microphone on the mixer desk and I just said, 'What the hell . . . I'll do it.' So I just picked up the mic and said 'Ladies and gentlemen . . . the New Barbarians!' and the show began. Richard said, 'Nice one—it's your job now.' And with that I was the one that introduced the band the rest of the tour."

As the Barbarians were no longer an opening act, they shifted into playing their full set, which would rarely vary during their 18 proper tour shows, from Ann Arbor to San Diego, 29 days in all. The band's songlist ran some one and a half hours, ranging from rock 'n' roll to blues, country to reggae, plus the odd Stones "cover."

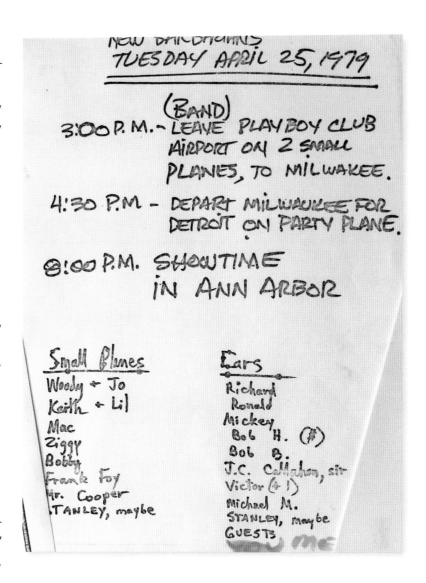

BARBARIANS ON A SCHEDULE
The handwritten schedule for the band's first show, at Ann Arbor, Michigan, on 24 April 1979. The Barbarians were right on schedule—but on the wrong date, as this was incorrectly dated "April 25." Gary Greenberg collection

BARBARIANS ITINERARY
(Overleaf) The official schedule posted for all Barbarians—musicians and crew members. Curt Angeledes collection

the *New Barbarians Go Eo...*

Toronto
BOUND:
Please take
the time to
assure that
you will be
clean upon
arrival.
Skip the soap
and go right
for the
vacuum.

15 April 1979	**16**	**17** Rehearsal at Culver City	**18** Rehearsal at Culver City
22 TORONTO Oshawa Civic Auditorium 2 shows SUN ✓	**23** OFF MON	**24** Ann Arbor Chrysler Arena ✓ TUE	**25** OFF WED
29 Milwaukee ARENA ✓	**30** Chicago Ampitheatre ✓	**1 May** OFF	**2** Pittsburg Civic Are... ✓
6 OFF	**7** NEW YORK CITY ✓ Madison Square Garden	**8** CLEVELAND ✓ Richfield Coliseum	**9** OFF
13 ✓ FORT WORTH Tarrant County Conv. Center	**14** OFF	**15** Denver ✓ McNichols Arena Band moves to L.A. after show	**16** OFF

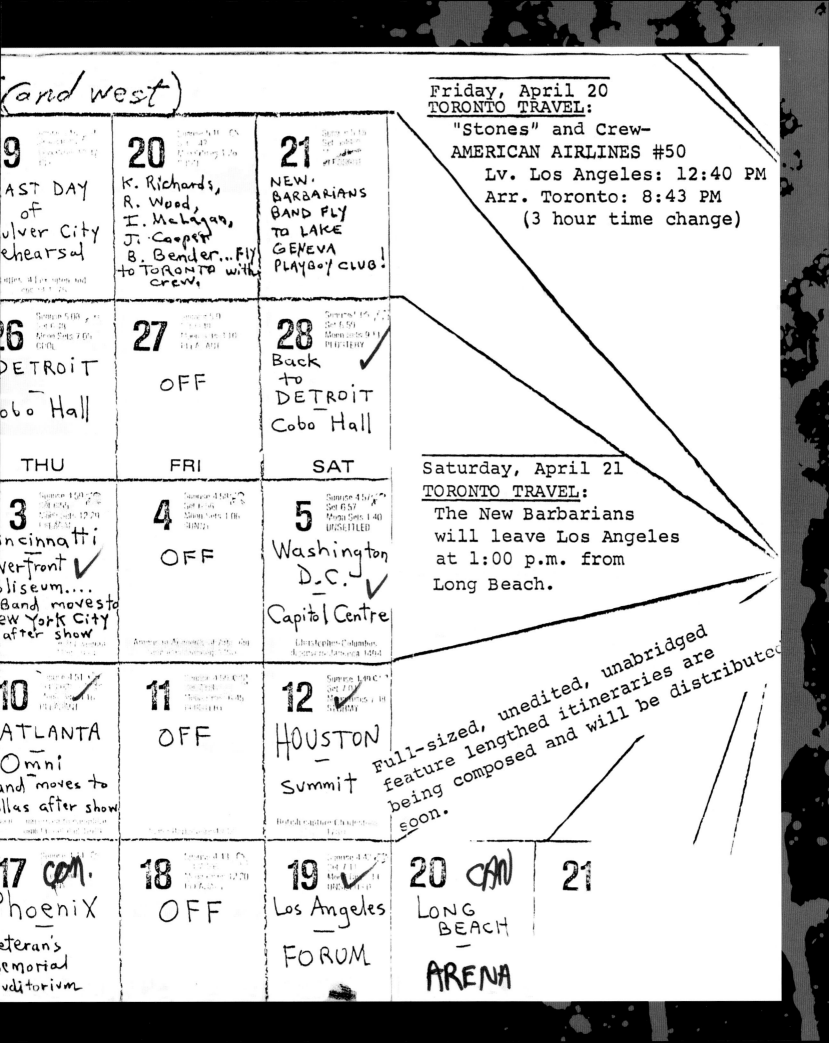

(and west)

19	20	21
LAST DAY of Culver City Rehearsal	K. Richards, R. Wood, I. McLagan, J. Cooper B. Bender...FLY to TORONTO with crew.	NEW BARBARIANS BAND FLY TO LAKE GENEVA PLAYBOY CLUB!
26 DETROIT Cobo Hall	27 OFF	28 ✓ Back to DETROIT Cobo Hall

THU	FRI	SAT
3 Cincinnatti Riverfront Coliseum.... Band moves to New York City after show ✓	4 OFF	5 Washington D.C. ✓ Capitol Centre
10 ✓ ATLANTA Omni Band moves to Dallas after show	11 OFF	12 ✓ HOUSTON - Summit
17 CAN. Phoenix Veteran's Memorial Auditorium	18 OFF	19 ✓ Los Angeles FORUM
	20 CAN LONG BEACH - ARENA	21

Friday, April 20
TORONTO TRAVEL:
  "Stones" and Crew—
AMERICAN AIRLINES #50
  Lv. Los Angeles: 12:40 PM
  Arr. Toronto: 8:43 PM
  (3 hour time change)

Saturday, April 21
TORONTO TRAVEL:
  The New Barbarians
  will leave Los Angeles
  at 1:00 p.m. from
  Long Beach.

Full-sized, unedited, unabridged
feature lengthed itineraries are
being composed and will be distributed
soon.

ANN ARBOR, 24 APRIL 1979

Let there be blood: Ken Graham's red stage swathed in red lights, as the Barbarians began their rampage.
Robert Alford

ANN ARBOR, 24 APRIL 1979

(Opposite) As Ronnie told *Mojo* decades later, "I never considered being the frontman. I think it was because I was the youngest member of every band I've been in. So it was always, 'My day will come.'" Robert Matheu

Ronnie opened each show with those classic Chuck Berry double-stops played on his Zemaitis, introducing "Sweet Little Rock & Roller," damn the torpedoes, full speed ahead. They then rolled straight into two of his own rockers from *Gimme Some Neck*: "Buried Alive" and "F.U.C. Her" powered by Woody and Keith's bourbon-soaked guitar licks over the taut, sleek backbeat. From there, the band settled into Woody's most beautiful ballad, "Mystifies Me." While the order of songs varied from show to show, they often then ramped the tempo back up for "Infekshun."

"Much of the time the vocals are inaudible, but nobody seems to mind," reported the *Post*. "They are enchanted by Richards, leaning forward from the hips like a marionette, feet rolled in on the arches, guitar hanging nearly to his knees: and by Clarke, feet planted solidly, two-thirds leg."

"THERE WAS A LOT OF TESTOSTERONE ON THAT STAGE!"

— STANLEY CLARKE

ANN ARBOR, 24 APRIL 1979
For the first night's encore, Ronnie came back on stage sporting a New Barbarians T-shirt that was suitably torn and frayed. Robert Matheu

For his part, Clarke describes the music simply: "There was a lot of testosterone on that stage!"

"Rock Me Baby" came next—a blues classic with a typical blues lineage: variations of the song had been cut by Lil' Son Jackson, Big Bill Broonzy, Arthur "Big Boy" Crudup, Muddy Waters, and likely others, although the Barbarians based their cover on B.B. King's 1964 version. Then they got real deep, playing the Jagger/Richards rocker "Sure The One You Need," which Keith had contributed to *I've Got My Own Album to Do*.

"The sound is full and relaxed," wrote Charles Shaar Murray in *New Musical Express*. "It isn't pompous overblown stadium rock and it isn't razor-edged British R&B, but it has that perfect combination of ease and power, lurch and balance, that characterises what is meant when the term 'barroom rock and roll' is used as a compliment."

Next up was *Gimme Some Neck*'s "Lost and Lonely," followed by "Breathe On Me" from *Now Look*. The Barbarians then stepped way back to Robert Johnson haunted "Love In Vain" from 1937, which the Stones covered on *Let It Bleed*. While the Stones' acoustic version was closer in mood to Johnson's, Keith now played it on his Telecaster, his six-string like a six-shooter, adding overdriven volume to the howl of the lyrics with Woody's bottleneck echoing his vocal lines.

"Let's Go Steady Again" was a Sam Cooke B side from 1959 penned by J. W. Alexander; Keith sang the slow song—a true vocal challenge—backed by Bobby Keys and Ronnie, making up a two-sax horn section. "Variety you want? Variety you get!" Wood announced to the crowd. As he remembered in his autobiography, "I suppose this goes back to my days in Yiewsley [where he grew up in the

ANN ARBOR, 24 APRIL 1979
The band may have been new at playing together, but they began to build a vibe right from the beginning, as Stanley Clarke remembers.
Robert Alford

London borough of Hillingdon]. I would spend every moment I could picking up instruments that were laying around the house. I pick up stuff very fast, so if you leave me alone with an instrument for a day or two, I'll figure out how to play something on it. . . . It was a two-week deal with the sax. I picked it up, learnt the scales and started to get the feel of it. I didn't know what the hell I was doing, except the sounds were coming out. . . . Well, you can imagine Keith's reaction. 'What the fuck are you doing with that?' I said, 'I'll show you.'" And show him he did.

Even Mac agreed that Woody was a fine hornsman: "Bobby had been showing him the basics. He practised every day, and was an incredibly quick learner."

Keith would then take a seat at the grand piano and sing Bobby Austin and Johnny Paycheck's country tearjerker "Apartment #9," which had been Tammy Wynette's first hit, back in '67. The song had

ANN ARBOR, 24 APRIL 1979
Ronnie and Keith find
their groove. Robert Alford

BARBARIAN FAMILY PORTRAIT
The band poses for a backstage picture in the bowels of Chicago's International Amphitheater on 30 April 1979. Robert Matheu

been part of Richards' solo Toronto sessions in '77, but now included Ronnie's pedal-steel fills. They continued the countrified vein with a grinding "Honky Tonk Women," sung by Woody.

"Worried Life Blues," the signature song of bluesman "Big Maceo" Merriweather, was another tune from Keith's Toronto sessions and first added to the setlist at the Pittsburgh show on 2 May. Woody's reggae rocker "I Can Feel the Fire" and mid-tempo "Come to Realise" followed. Ron then pulled out a harp and did his best Little Walter to accent Freddie Scott's "Am I Grooving You" and its slow, languorous groove.

It was at the tail end of "Grooving You" that most of the band retreated into that secret room at the back of the stage for refreshments, leaving Stanley Clarke and Ziggy alone onstage with a chance to step out. Fernandez: "During Ziggy and Stanley's solo, the others would go back into the secret room and smoke a joint or have a cigarette, have a couple drinks, and kibbitz about the music—like you know, 'Don't forget we changed the song and we're going to the G there.' Keith and Ronnie liked the secret room because it was a place they could go that was offstage but not truly *off*stage. It was a good little respite for them."

NEW BARBARIANS DUDS

Showco shirt from the Matt Lee collection; others Curt
Angeledes and Voyageur Press collections

Now it was Stanley and Ziggy's stage, and they blew the shows wide open. With cool and deadly ease, they did a duet solo—and their interplay was the musical highlight. Both of them pulled out any stops and dove into the R&B they both loved, syncopating each other's riffs and often surprising themselves. Stanley's funk-inspired, thumb-powered slaps and pops brought the crowd to a peak of frenzy each time and won him the laudatory label Jumpin' Black Flash from reviewers. He was part Bootsy Collins, part Jimi Hendrix—100,000 watts of pure Stanley Clarke.

Even the jaded crew—who had seen many a rock 'n' roll concert from the sidelines—was wowed. Fernandez: "Seeing Stanley Clarke and Ziggy work together—un-*fucking*-real! It was just like—*damn*!"

Recharged, the Barbarians reappeared from their secret room and dashed into Dylan's "Seven Days." Keith's "Before They Make Me Run" would finish the shows, often followed by a wide-full-open "Jumpin' Jack Flash" sung by Ronnie as a reprise or encore, depending on the night, leaving the crowds with a contagious case of Doctor Ross' boogie disease.

And with that, they disappeared—off to the champagne, M&Ms (both plain *and* peanut, according to the *Post*), and other comforts of the 727 on their way back to the Playboy Club. Their departure was consummately choreographed, a moment of sheer corps de ballet perfection, reported the *Post*: "Within 30 seconds of the last chord, all five limos are loaded and moving out—a manager's dream." And remembers Stanley, "After the gig, there was no messing around: We'd come off the stage and go right into a limousine and they'd take us to the plane and we'd fly back to our hotel—and be up all night groovin'." Ronnie would often sit down to dinner—at 5:30 in the morning, as the *Washington Post* witnessed. The Barbarians were living purely on rock 'n' roll time, flipping the clock upside down, swapping a.m.'s for p.m.'s, and happily embracing unreality.

With the Barbarians, Ronnie Wood and Co. refined the modern rock 'n' roll tour. Thanks in large part to concerns over entering Canada following Keith's '77 heroin arrest, they devised the logistics to set up a homebase in a luxury hotel neighboring an airport runway, then travel by chartered jet—instead of busing it or even flying from city to city, hotel to hotel in a day-after-day marathon slog as Led Zeppelin had done in the same 727, or as the Stones did on their tours. Semi trucks and buses drove the gear, stage, and crew to meet them. Only the best wines and imported beer were served, and the crew didn't have to suffer with just cold cuts for dinner; they were instead served hot prime rib with all the trimmings. And there was no need to trash hotel rooms, because there's no stress or

DETROIT, 26 APRIL 1979
Barbarian fare. Henry Diltz

DETROIT, 26 APRIL 1979
One of Ronnie Wood's fave pictures from the Barbarians tour. Robert Matheu

DETROIT, 28 APRIL 1979

(Left) The man in black: Keith picks his five-stringed '54 Telecaster "Micawber," that was one of his main guitars throughout the Barbarians' reign. Keith: "There's no reason for my guitar being called Micawber, apart from the fact that it's such an unlikely name [taken from Charles Dickens' *David Copperfield*]. There's no one around me called Micawber, so, when I scream for Micawber, everyone knows what I'm talking about."
Robert Matheu

DETROIT, 28 APRIL 1979

(Right) Bobby Keys and Ronnie harmonize on saxes on "Let's Go Steady Again." "Variety you want? Variety you get!" Ronnie would tell audiences. Robert Matheu

CINCINNATI, 3 MAY 1979

(Opposite) Show pass.
Matt Lee collection

frustration: Helium-bloated egos bumping into each other backstage were happily absent, and a stately, low-key consideration prevailed. The hordes of groupies had given way to the steady girlfriends who traveled with Wood, Richards, and others. Monies were calculated every day and the books were open to band members at all times, by Ronnie's order. And they were spending money gloriously. Which was exactly how Ronnie had planned it: "I wanted to do this in style," he told the *Post*. And there was less fear of drug busts along the way. The grand rock 'n' roll tour had come of age.

Ziggy remembers the tour and the band culture fondly: "I had already seen the way the Stones were living out there [on the road]. The Meters, we were just like any other R&B group: Those booking agents had us going through all of the Chitlin Circuit—you played auditoriums, theaters, clubs. With the Rolling Stones, it was like a city traveling, with three floors of hotel rooms, everything blocked off, five-star hotels—it's living at a certain level. I used to wonder to myself, *How do people stay on the road that long, away from their loved ones and family, it's gotta be some something difficult to do?* I found out those cats were doing it the way it was always supposed to be done. Their family was out there with them. And wherever they were on the road, when people needed to talk to them about the shows, the routing, whatever, it all came to them. It made a huge difference. Those people knew how to go first class, and that's really a terrific thing for the mindset of any artist."

BARBARIANS AT THE GATE: OFFICIAL TOUR DATES

Sunday, 22 April 1979: two shows opening for the Rolling Stones at Oshawa Civic Auditorium, Oshawa, Ontario

Tuesday, 24 April 1979: Crisler Arena, Ann Arbor, Michigan

Thursday, 26 April 1979: Cobo Arena, Detroit, Michigan

Saturday, 28 April 1979: Cobo Arena, Detroit, Michigan

Sunday, 29 April 1979: Milwaukee Arena, Milwaukee, Wisconsin

Monday, 30 April 1979: International Amphitheater, Chicago, Illinois

Wednesday, 2 May 1979: Civic Arena, Pittsburgh, Pennsylvania

Thursday, 3 May 1979: Riverfront Coliseum, Cincinnati, Ohio (move base to New York City after the show)

Saturday, 5 May 1979: Capital Centre Arena, Largo, Maryland (Washington, D.C.)

Monday, 7 May 1979: Madison Square Garden, New York, New York

Tuesday, 8 May 1979: Richfield Coliseum, Richfield (Cleveland), Ohio

Thursday, 10 May 1979: Omni Coliseum, Atlanta, Georgia (move base to Dallas after the show)

Saturday, 12 May 1979: The Summit, Houston, Texas

Sunday, 13 May 1979: Tarrant County Convention Center, Fort Worth, Texas

Tuesday, 15 May 1979: McNichols Arena, Denver, Colorado (move base to Los Angeles after show)

Thursday, 17 May 1979: Salt Palace, Salt Lake City, Utah

Saturday, 19 May 1979: The Forum, Los Angeles, California

Sunday, 20 May 1979: Oakland–Alameda County Coliseum, Oakland, California

Tuesday, 22 May 1979: San Diego Sports Arena, San Diego, California

11 August 1979: Knebworth Festival, Knebworth, England

16 January 1980: Uptown Theater, Milwaukee, Wisconsin

Other shows were also originally planned but canceled or changed at the last moment. These other shows included:

Thursday, 26 April 1979: St. Louis, Missouri

Thursday, 10 May 1979: Birmingham, Alabama

Wednesday, 16 May 1979: Tucson, Arizona

Thursday, 17 May 1979: Phoenix, Arizona

Sunday, 20 May 1979: Long Beach, California

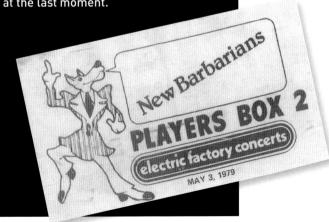

JUMPIN' BLACK FLASH
Stanley Clarke and Ziggy's solo spot was a highpoint of every show. As *Melody Maker* noted, "How many times have you seen an audience on its feet for a bass guitar solo?" Henry Diltz

DETROIT, 28 APRIL 1979

Ronnie and Keith share the spotlight.

Robert Matheu

DETROIT, 28 APRIL 1979

(Opposite) The Barbarians on the rampage. Robert Alford

All of which harkened back to Ronnie's initial concept of the New Barbarians: A vacation from the drudgery of what the guys did for a living—writing, playing their guitars, recording. As the official band itinerary read after the last show, "Back to real life." But during the tour, all was right with the world: As Ronnie told the *Post* with all the pious zealousness of a true believer, "Ah, it's great! It's only rock 'n' roll."

"AFTER THE GIG, THERE WAS NO MESSING AROUND: WE'D COME OFF THE STAGE AND GO RIGHT INTO A LIMOUSINE AND THEY'D TAKE US TO THE PLANE AND WE'D FLY BACK TO OUR HOTEL—AND BE UP ALL NIGHT GROOVIN'."

— STANLEY CLARKE

"AH, IT'S GREAT! IT'S ONLY ROCK 'N' ROLL."

— RONNIE WOOD

CHAPTER 7
NO ONE HERE
BUT US CHICKENS

WHO THE FUCK ARE THE NEW BARBARIANS?

— IAN MCLAGAN'S CUSTOM-MADE T-SHIRT

CHICAGO, 1 MAY 1979
(Opposite) Ron Wood gets low down.
Kirk West/Getty Images

Inset Curt Angeledes collection

Not all fans thought the rock 'n' roll was as great as they were led to expect, though. At many Barbarian shows, the band was at moments almost drowned out by chanted demands from the crowds. The first times this occurred, Ronnie was bemused, then confused, and ultimately not amused.

"We'd be up there rocking and the crowds would be shouting, 'Where's Bob? Where's Mick?' I'd shout back, 'What?' They'd shout, 'Where's Jagger?' I'd shout back, 'What the fuck are you talking about?' They'd shout, 'Where's Dylan?' I'd be up there trying to play music and talk to 20,000 people who thought they were going to see Mick and Bob. 'What you see is what you get.'"

Or, as Ronnie grew fond of telling the crowds, "Contrary to what you've heard, there ain't no

"WHAT YOU SEE IS WHAT YOU GET."

— RONNIE WOOD

"WHO THE FUCK ARE THE NEW BARBARIANS?"
Mac—ever the joker—models his own custom Barbarians T-shirt while Bobby Keys looks skeptical. Henry Diltz

. . . AND FRIENDS
(Opposite) Concert poster for the Pittsburgh show on 2 May 1979. The promise of "friends" meant different things to different people—and was part of what spurred expectation of seeing guest stars, from Jagger to Rod Stewart to Dylan. Furthermore, just who was this "Ian McLaughlin"? "Stanley Clark"? "Bobby Keyes"? Why wasn't Ziggy mentioned? And why did Keith Richards get top billing over bandleader, solo artist, sugar daddy, and all-around evil genius Ron Wood?

WEDNESDAY NIGHT

THE NEW BARBARIANS

FEATURING

KEITH RICHARDS
&
RON WOOD

OF THE ROLLING STONES

&
FRIENDS

Stanley Clark, Ian McLaughlin, & Bobby Keyes

MAY 2   8PM   CIVIC ARENA

General & Reserved Seats Available

Available at all   National Record Mart
Stores and the   Arena box office

©1999 MVS. 500 Ltd — 2 posters

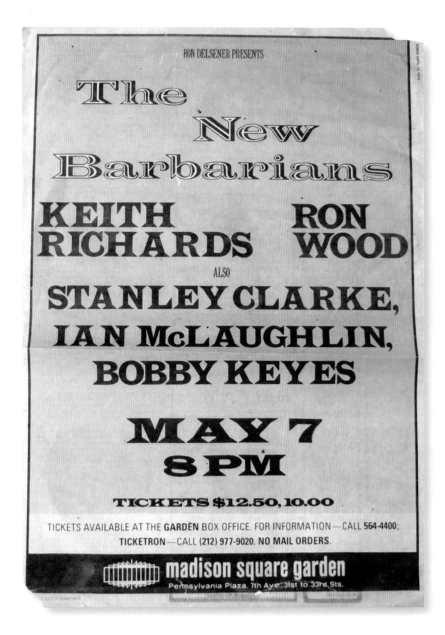

RON DELSENER PRESENTS

The New Barbarians

KEITH RICHARDS   RON WOOD

ALSO

STANLEY CLARKE,
IAN McLAUGHLIN,
BOBBY KEYES

MAY 7
8 PM

TICKETS $12.50, 10.00

TICKETS AVAILABLE AT THE **GARDEN** BOX OFFICE. FOR INFORMATION—CALL 564-4400;
TICKETRON—CALL (212) 977-9020. NO MAIL ORDERS.

madison square garden
Pennsylvania Plaza. 7th Ave. 31st to 33rd Sts.

**MADISON SQUARE GARDEN,
7 MAY 1979**
(Above) Newspaper advertisement.

Gary Greenberg collection

one here but us chickens. There are no special guests tonight . . . except you lot!"

In his autobiography, Keys remembered: "Usually you could kinda take it for granted at this point in time that people were gonna like you, but the audience was clearly not as receptive as they normally were. Plus, they kept hollering out, 'Where's Bob? Where's Bob?' I remember thinking, *Well, right here*. We had no idea what was going on. It was really, really confusing. The whole thing was a drag, and the papers really slammed every-body, and it pissed Keith off to the point of distraction."

"Who the Fuck Are the New Barbarians?" read the T-shirt as sported by Ian McLagan for fun and fashion. The question was posed in jest, but several peo-ple say that Woody's manager Jason Cooper had been secretly asking it in all seriousness. He reportedly had his doubts that even two Rolling Stones and their musical party-on-wheels could fill concert halls. And they were big concert halls—a seat sold is a seat sold. So he cultivated rumors among journalists and deejays, who excitedly spread the word. Depending on the locale, they had it on good authority—about the best, most trusted authority they could wish for—that guests at the upcoming New Barbarians show would include Bob Dylan, Mick Jagger, Rod Stewart, Jimmy Page, Peter Frampton. The list went on. Announcing the tour, *Rolling Stone* said it, and so it must be; this was the bible of rock 'n' roll at the time, and more trustworthy when it came to "The Music" than the *New York Times* in the fans' eyes. Even the rumors didn't agree with each other: The *Washington Post* added David Bowie, Ringo Starr, Bob Seger, and Dickie Betts to the list; Lindsay Buckingham and David Crosby's names were also whispered out loud. Others mention Joe Walsh.

And the gig posters were coy about it, hinting discreetly that the two Stones would be joined by "Friends."

And so ticketholders believed they were holding one special ticket. They came to the shows, duly waited out the Barbarians' Chuck Berry covers, soul classics, and Ronnie's tunes, expecting to see the Big Names.

And the Big Names didn't show. Ever. They were never going to in the first place.

The fans weren't getting no satisfaction, and so the Barbarians' shows were often interrupted by the crowds' chants for the Big Names. And when the special guests were not forthcoming, trouble was.

Ascertaining who did what to whom at the different shows is impossible, and in truth there was probably more bark than bite. But at many a show, there were indeed toothmarks left in the wake.

Right from the start, at the Ann Arbor show, rumors that Jagger would appear didn't come true, and the crowd was vocal in their

**MADISON SQUARE GARDEN,
7 MAY 1979**

Ziggy behind his kit: "I had opened up for the Stones all over America and Europe—you can't get no bigger than that. But this had a special meaning." Ebet Roberts

**MADISON SQUARE GARDEN,
7 MAY 1979**

(Overleaf) "There ain't no one here but us chickens," Ronnie began telling audiences who called out for Jagger, Rod Stewart, or any other rumored guest stars. Richard E. Aaron/Redferns/ Getty Images

**MADISON SQUARE GARDEN,
7 MAY 1979**
(Left) Ron and Keith sing to the
faithful. Ebet Roberts

**MADISON SQUARE GARDEN,
7 MAY 1979**
(Right) Keith and Micawber roll out
"Jumpin' Jack Flash." Ebet Roberts

disappointment. During the 26 and 28 April shows at Detroit's Cobo
Arena, the crowd's catcalls got even louder.

It was at the Sunday night concert on 29 April at the Mecca
Arena in wholesome, Midwestern Milwaukee that things got out of
hand. At the end of "Jumpin' Jack Flash," angered fans charged the
stage, only to be forced back by police; the scuffle turned into a
"mêlée," as described by *Billboard*, and fans smashed wooden chairs
and broke the arena's windows. As the Barbarians headed for their
727, the police arrested 81 concertgoers: 15 were charged with various offenses including fighting and vandalism.

That was just the start. Threats of lawsuits ensued from both
the Milwaukee district attorney, who started investigating whether
fraudulent advertising charges would be filed against the concert

promoters, and the Wisconsin attorney general, who was examining whether radio ads on WQFM and WLPX were deceptive.

This prompted the promoters to bicker over who was to blame. The local Milwaukee promoter, Landmark Production, headed by Alan Dulberger, pointed the finger at the Barbarians' manager, Jason Cooper, and International Creative Management (ICM), the tour promoter, according to reports in the *Milwaukee Journal* and *Milwaukee Sentinel*.

Dulberger protested his innocence as part of a back-and-forth war of words in the press: "I was informed by ICM that I should advertise to the public that there was going to be a surprise guest. Many names were mentioned to me. However, I was informed not to specify the name of any surprise guest because ICM was not sure who the special guests would be at the time."

MADISON SQUARE GARDEN, 7 MAY 1979

(Left) Ronnie with his special Tony Zemaitis metal-front "Custom Ron Wood 1978" guitar, featuring engravings of American themes and built initially for the Stones' '78 North American tour. Ebet Roberts

MADISON SQUARE GARDEN, 7 MAY 1979

(Right) Keith plays frontman, belting out "Before They Make Me Run." Ebet Roberts

MADISON SQUARE GARDEN, 7 MAY 1979
(Above) Ronnie does some mighty fine Chuck Berry moves. <small>Ebet Roberts</small>

MADISON SQUARE GARDEN, 7 MAY 1979
(Opposite) Keith slings his black-on-black '75 Telecaster Custom, which would be one of his main guitars throughout the tour. <small>Ebet Roberts</small>

Cooper denied this. "We just never have any idea who's going to show up. Whenever the promoter asks who's going to show up, we tell him we never know. It's almost the nature of the business."

"Almost" being the key word.

ICM's senior booking agent, John Marx, then admitted telling Landmark that two guests were coming—Jeff Beck and Jimmy Page—but later found out that they wouldn't show. It was unclear whether he passed that news along.

"We feel terrible that it happened," Cooper went on. "If we would have done one more encore, it wouldn't have happened. But Ron Wood's back was hurting and we had to leave. The kids just got all excited."

"WE JUST NEVER HAVE ANY IDEA WHO'S GOING TO SHOW UP. WHENEVER THE PROMOTER ASKS WHO'S GOING TO SHOW UP, WE TELL HIM WE NEVER KNOW. IT'S ALMOST THE NATURE OF THE BUSINESS."

— JASON COOPER

PLAYING THE BLUES

The crowd's expectations for guest stars at the Barbarians' shows were realized at last at the 30 April concert at Chicago's International Amphitheater, which featured a special, unannounced guest—Chicago blues mainstay Junior Wells.

On the Stones' 1970 European tour, Wells and Buddy Guy had been the opening act, often threatening the headliners with their fiery, intense performances. Now, after the Barbarians hit the final notes of "Love In Vain" in Chicago, Wells was announced. (Guy was also supposed to appear at the International Amphitheater, but was driving north from New Orleans and missed the gig.)

Wells powered the Barbarians through "Key To The Highway," Big Bill Broonzy's hit song that Wells and Guy often played together: this was the version Derek mined on *Layla and Other Assorted Love Songs* that made the song known to rock 'n' rollers. They then rolled into Wells' trademark tune "Hoodoo Man Blues," a deep, slow lament spiced by Woody and Richards' guitars.

Keith Richards in particular was not happy with the situation. As Stanley remembers, "I remember them tearing the hall up. Keith was pretty angry."

He was even angrier with Jason Cooper, a jovial, ginger-bearded giant, ex-footballer nicknamed "Moke." Keith never liked Cooper, according to multiple sources, and this was the final straw. Cooper had been Dave Mason's manager—which helped explain Mason's appearance on *Gimme Some Neck*—but things had now gotten out of hand; as Gary Schultz explains, "Managing a tour with a couple of the Rolling Stones was a different matter."

There are various versions of what happened next: Memories are clouded by the adrenaline of the moment, time, and maybe other things. Stanley remembers sitting with security man Michael Mauer on the 727 after the show when Ronnie came running down the aisle, calling for help—"Keith's pissed off and he's pointing a .44-magnum pistol at Jason," he remembers Ronnie shouting. Others remember it being a switchblade, but either way, the intent was clear. The situation was defused, with the result that Jason Cooper was off the tour and out of a job.

Keys: "When Keith found out what had happened and how come the papers were saying all these bad things, he grabbed Jason Cooper and put a knife to his throat and told him to get the fuck out and if he saw him again he was gonna put a bullet between his eyes. And you know what? There was a helicopter out there to Wisconsin within thirty minutes. He was on that helicopter and he was gone and we never saw him again. There are some things you just don't do."

Meanwhile, the legal hassles in Milwaukee were amping up. A class-action lawsuit was filed seeking up to $200,000 in damages plus restitution to ticketholders who felt they'd been misled. And everyone involved was going to be charged for damages to the arena. On May 3, the state attorney general found that the promotion of Big Names at the show was "unduly suggestive and deceptive."

In the end, it became a *legal* mêlée, and it was only settled thanks to an agreement that ironically mirrored in concept Keith's benefit concert for the blind in Toronto: The New Barbarians would return to Milwaukee to play a court-ordered make-up show to cover the costs for all involved.

Seven months later, on 16 January 1980, Ronnie was back at Milwaukee's Uptown Theater with a band that in name and spirit continued on the legacy of the New Barbarians of '79. Most of the original band had dispersed, but Mac was back on keyboards alongside Bobby Keys, but others musicians filled out the group: guitarman

BARBARIAN PASSES

Gary Greenberg collection

"IT WAS LIKE WHERE THE VILLAGERS RIOTED IN AN OLD *FRANKENSTEIN* MOVIE."

— KEN GRAHAM

Johnny Lee Schell formerly of Texan Southern rock band Baby, one-time Sly and the Family Stone drummer Andy Newmark, and bass-ist Reggie McBride replaced Keith, Ziggy, and Stanley. MacKenzie Phillips—teen star of *American Graffiti* and TV's *One Day at a Time* and daughter of the Mamas and the Papas' John Phillips—sang back-ing vocals and added star power.

By the time of the original Milwaukee court settlement, though, the Barbarians were long gone. After the 3 May show at Cincinnati's Riverfront Coliseum, the band decamped from the Playboy Club and moved its base of operations to New York City's Mayfair Hotel for the East Coast leg of the tour: Largo, Maryland, on the edge of Washington, D.C., on 5 May, Madison Square Garden on 7 May, Cleveland on 8 May, and Atlanta on 10 May.

And the angry crowds continued as well. The barnstorming tour turned into barn burnings. There was another near riot in Cincinnati, where Ronnie desperately tried to settle the audience.

At Madison Square Garden, things turned ugly again. Ken Graham explains: "The Barbarians knew X amount of songs and they wouldn't come back for an encore and the set was less than an hour and thirty minutes. At Madison Square Garden, the fans were *pissed*. They got a short show, they got no encore, and they got no special guests—especially no Mick Jagger."

More innocent chairs suffered a sad fate as the crowd smashed and threw them. Graham and soundman Buford T. Jones used their bodies to block the mixing board from the flying furniture. Graham remembers the scene: "It was like where the villagers rioted in an old *Frankenstein* movie."

The actual Barbarians, however, had already left the building.

CHAPTER 8
RIP THIS JOINT

"WHO THE FUCK IS MICK JAGGER?"

— FAMOUS 1970s T-SHIRT

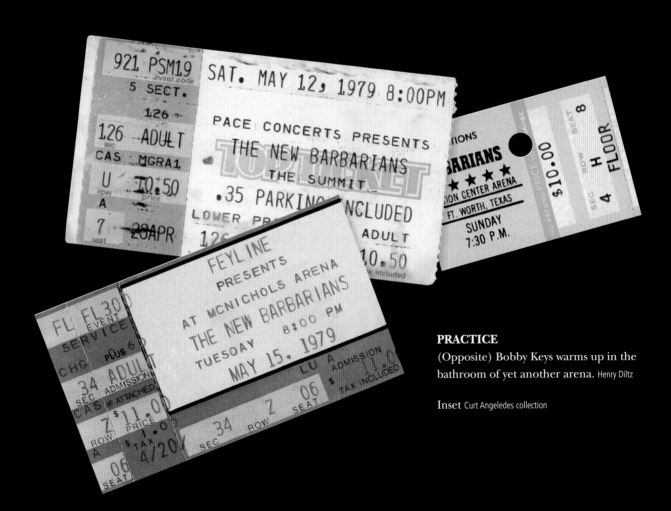

PRACTICE

(Opposite) Bobby Keys warms up in the
bathroom of yet another arena. Henry Diltz

Inset Curt Angeledes collection

JAMMING

Whether it was an ancient blues, a rock 'n' roll classic, a Stones tune, one of Ronnie's numbers, or just a made-up riff, it didn't matter: The band members loved to play. Houston, 12 May 1979. Henry Diltz

Ronnie Wood and Keith Richards went together like drunk and disorderly. When the Barbarians were on stage, they were a band of brothers. When they were off stage, the fun only got louder—which is saying a lot, considering their stage volume.

It began backstage before each show, an impromptu jam session that turned into a ritual. The band members pulled out their instruments and tuned up. Sometimes they played acoustically, other times they'd plug in to their petite Pignose or small Mesa Boogie combo amps. And they'd pick old blues numbers, their own songs, or just make something up and see where it took them. It formed a musical bond between them. And they couldn't get enough.

When it was showtime, Richard Fernandez says, "I'd have to come up and grab Ronnie's shoulder and say, 'Hey, pal, everybody's ready to go up on stage.' And they'd ignore me. So the the first few shows, I'd try to get Ronnie's attention and say, 'Hey, we're on! We're on!'

"I had to play all sorts of games—give them a fake count-down, tell them we're going on in 10 minutes when we had 20 minutes to go. They'd some-times look at me and say, 'Long 10 minutes!' And I'd grin and say, 'Yeah, long 10 minutes.'

"About three shows into the tour, I went to grab Ronnie, and said, 'Let's go, let's go!' Then I happened to look over and make eye contact with Keith, and he immediately unplugged his guitar and said, 'We're on!'— and everyone stopped playing and went on stage. So I realized, *Ha, that's how you get these guys onstage*!"

While it was without doubt Ron's band, Keith was the elder statesman that everyone looked up to, including Ronnie. Fernandez: "From the very beginning, I always felt like Keith was like Ronnie's older brother, making sure he didn't get fucked over in any way. Ronnie was definitely the man in charge, but he'd often coun-sel with Keith. Ronnie had a lot of responsibility on his shoul-ders. I'm not going to say he was more focused than on the Faces or Stones tours, but he was more concerned. He would often defer to Keith and powwow with Keith, whether it was a musical or man-agement decision. Ronnie really wanted to make it good for every-body. Everybody messed around, but when it came to work, Keith was there, 100 percent."

Ronnie was the master of ceremonies, the frontman, the band-leader, the sugar daddy—the evil genius. But Keith was Keith, and respect was due. And Keith played like he rarely played. In past years he had looked ever more impossibly ghoulish and voluptuously

JAM SESSION

Backstage before shows, the Barbarians made a ritual out of jamming, as here in their dressing room at The Summit in Houston on 12 May 1979, with a line of Mesa Boogie amps providing the power.

Henry Diltz

SHOWTIME

(Above and opposite) The Barbarians jam backstage before their Fort Worth show on 13 May 1979—until tour manager Richard Fernandez (in his trademark white hat) interrupts the proceedings to get the band onstage in time. Henry Diltz

moribund. He had almost literally come back from the dead—and he looked happy to be alive. His confidante Gary Schultz says, "After years of heroin, it dulls your sexual desire. Off of heroin and having cleaned his body up, he had a girlfriend who was the best friend of Ronnie's girlfriend and so Keith was smiling from ear to ear, musically and after the show as well."

Keith even had a new and improved smile to prove it. As part of his campaign of self-development, he announced, "I'm changing my image; I'm finally getting my teeth fixed." Now, during his time off after the Toronto bust, his dentures morphed from gnarly black to pearly white. "Miraculously, due to abstinence and prayer, my teeth grew back!" he joked with *Melody Maker*'s Chris Welch: "I think I was just late developing. Nothing an expensive operation couldn't prolong."

As Keith wrote in his autobiography: "It was a fun tour and we had a lot of laughs. I didn't have to worry about the things I usually do on tours; I didn't have to bear responsibility. To me, it was a ball,

a riot. I was basically just a sideman hired for the tour. I can't even remember much of it, it was so much fun. To me, the important thing was that, shit, I'd managed to avoid doing hard time, and at the same time I was doing what I love to do."

The band as a whole sensed this. And that upped the ante musically as well.

Gary Schultz says, "The Barbarians were really special. You have a rhythm section like Stanley Clarke and Zigaboo—they were *solid*, a motor, it was really beautiful. And the guitars of Keith and Ronnie meshed well with Stanley. Then Ian McLagan and Bobby Keys—there was nothing like them. They were a special band. They enjoyed playing together, and whenever that happens, you can feel it. It was evident that it was *really* working."

Fernandez: "The musicians got along fabulously. They all came from such different places, but there was no weirdness there at all. The guys were driving between the white lines. They were doing it. They were really into it. The camaraderie and what they were

"FOR A LITTLE BIT OF TIME SIX OF US GOT LOST IN THE MUSIC."

— RONNIE WOOD

THE JET SET
Playtime began on the airplane to the concerts: As Chuch attempts to grab some needed rest, Keith and Mac josh around while Jason Cooper looks on.
Henry Diltz

doing onstage—they all seemed to want to pull it off. And with that caliber of musicians, it was an extraordinary scene. I'd look around at them and think, *Whoa, we've got some heavy cats here! This is the shit!"*

Ronnie, too, understood, as he remembered in his autobiography: "For a little bit of time six of us got lost in the music."

And the Barbarians were properly loud.

It began with Stanley: "I had an Alembic bass, which is what I always used, and at that point I was using EV [Electro-Voice] cabinets. But Ronnie had four [Ampeg] SVTs for me because he liked a really strong stage sound for the bass. It was just *pounding*—you could kill a bird if it flew across the stage. It was nice to hear the sound so big."

Ronnie and Keith were also backed by a wall of power. Ronnie's solos were deep-throated, while Keith's often cut through the band with a trebly edge. He might have reformed his life, but he remained a fire-and-brimstone atheist proudly preaching the gospel of loud.

RIDING SHOTGUN

(Left) Stanley doesn't remember where or why he came by this shotgun; perhaps it was a Texas souvenir. Henry Diltz

HOT STUFF

(Right) Ziggy models his fave hot sauce. Henry Diltz

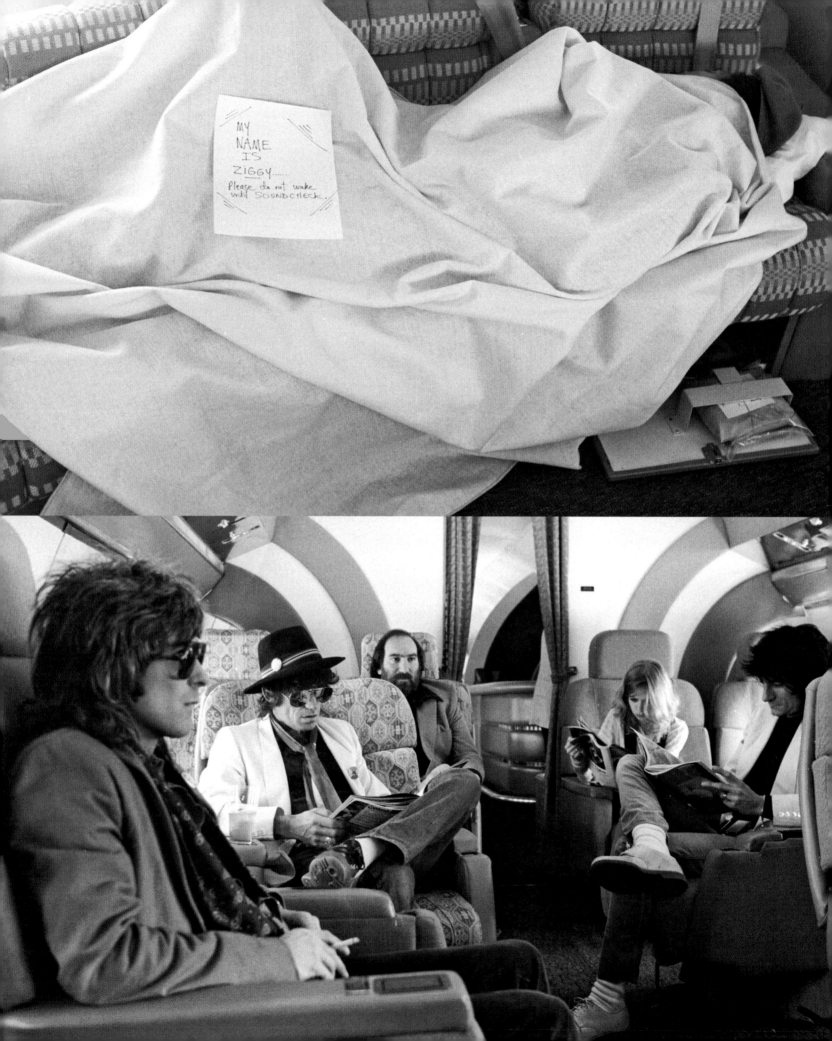

In fact, the band was often so powerful that the vocals got lost in the mix behind the instruments' volume. At times, their sound verged on being a musical trainwreck, but more often they came together with loose, unadorned, glorious rock 'n' roll the way it should be played.

That the Barbarians enjoyed making the music didn't mean they didn't enjoy themselves when they were off the job as well.

Remember that little room off the back of the stage? That was nothing, says Stanley Clarke: "There were a lot of 'little rooms' in a lot of places. There was a lot of X-rated stuff going on. It was a complete, 100-percent rock 'n' roll tour, the kind of thing you'd read about in the magazines—just what you think a rock 'n' roll tour should be. Everything was there, all the bells and whistles, all the perks, all the extras, all the ups and downs.

"There were drugs there, but surely they weren't the only guys on the planet doing drugs. There were a lot of bell bottoms, but I'd seen that. There were a lot of white guys with long hair and even afros, but I'd seen that too."

Many of the crew had worked with the Faces and later with the Stones, and they enjoyed drawing comparisons with the Barbarians. Fernandez: "The Faces were the best drunk band I've ever worked with—and I mean that in a good way, a fucking great way! Beside all being excellent musicians, it was like hanging out with Laurel and Hardy and Abbott and Costello all at the same time—and they happened to be some of the best rock musicians in the world. It was

SHUTEYE
(Opposite top) Ziggy sleeps. Henry Diltz

QUIET TIME
(Opposite bottom) En route to another show, the Barbarians use the plane ride to catch up on their reading. Henry Diltz

WELCOME TO L.A.
(Top) The Barbarians arrive in Los Angeles to unseasonably cold weather. Henry Diltz

RIDING IN STYLE
(Bottom) A lineup of limos greets the Barbarians to take them to their next show. Henry Diltz

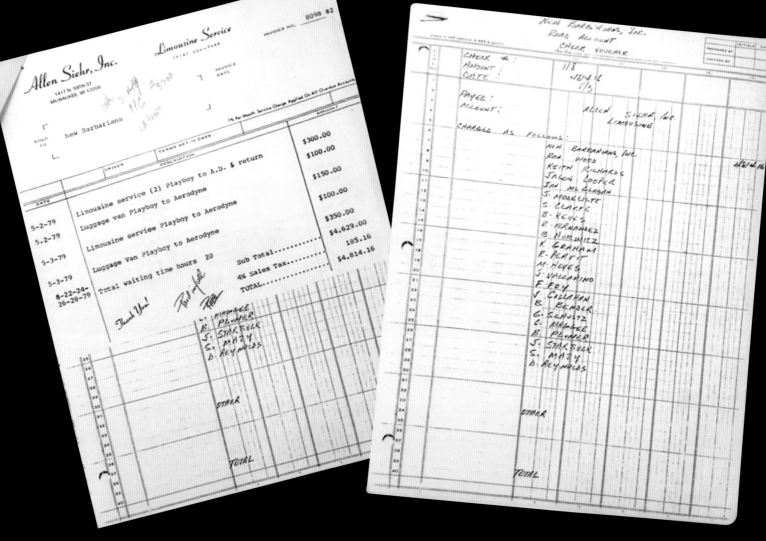

**LIMOUSINE SERVICE
PAPERWORK**

(Top) Matt Lee collection

HAPPY HOUR

(Bottom and opposite) Keeping
things well oiled. Henry Diltz

"IT WAS A COMPLETE, 100-PERCENT ROCK 'N' ROLL TOUR, THE KIND OF THING YOU'D READ ABOUT IN THE MAGAZINES—JUST WHAT YOU THINK A ROCK 'N' ROLL TOUR SHOULD BE. EVERYTHING WAS THERE, ALL THE BELLS AND WHISTLES, ALL THE PERKS, ALL THE EXTRAS, ALL THE UPS AND DOWNS."

— STANLEY CLARKE

"THE INMATES WERE IN CHARGE OF THE ASYLUM."

— JOHNNY STARBUCK

SECURITY

(Bottom) Jim Callahan—better known as J.C.—and Big Bob Bender guard the Barbarians dressing room. Henry Diltz

THE NICE-SMELLING BARBARIAN

(Opposite) Keith goes through his pre-show ablutions. Henry Diltz

constant jokes and pranks and ribbing of each other. The Faces were more a good-time band, the jovial guys straight out of the bar. They drank this really shitty Mateus rosé wine at first, and when we'd go to the Fillmore East, Bill Graham would announce, 'The Fillmore East and the Mateus Bottling Company proudly present the Faces!' and they'd go out on stage almost stumbling, then put their instruments on and just bang it out. One tour, we had a bar on stage, and Mickey Heyes was the bartender and the band members would come up to him and order a drink and he'd pour it and serve it to them as they played. I have the fondest memories of all that.

"The New Barbarians were a little more down to business, but they still had a lot of fun."

And Mick Jagger was nowhere in sight. He wasn't even present in spirit.

Johnny Starbuck: "The inmates were in charge of the asylum. Without anyone like Mick Jagger or a hard-nosed tour manager cracking the whip, it was just one long party. It was technically Ronnie's band, but it was Keith that was pretty much the leader. And when you're following his lead . . . well, you can just imagine. There were no rules."

As Bobby Keys simply said: "Son, that was a ton of fun." So much fun, in fact, that Stanley swears to this day that Keys never slept during the whole tour. . . but then again, "Maybe I slept at the same time Bobby did."

And while no hotel rooms got trashed, that didn't mean that rooms didn't *suffer*. Fernandez remembers one incident amidst the opulence and grandeur of Ronnie's suite at Manhattan's Mayfair Hotel. "Ronnie calls me up and he and Keith were in Ronnie's room and he asked for Mickey. 'I need him to go get me some more spraypaint,' Ronnie tells me. And I said, *OK* . . . Mickey came to me and he said, 'Richard, you gotta go down there.' I headed down there and Ronnie and Keith were painting one of Woody's

guitars and case—in the bathroom in one of these grand hotels in New York City. My only thought was, *Oh no, how much is this going to cost us?!* But they were deep into it and having a great time. It just cracked me up."

To Stanley, coming from the jazz world, it was a little . . . rambunctious, although he swears he never suffered culture shock. The cool jazz guy amidst the rock 'n' roll Barbarians, he'd seen a lot. Still, he hadn't seen it all.

Stanley: "I was a bit of a health nut at that point, and Keith came onto the plane and he was looking pretty grim. I don't know what was going on with him but he said to me, 'Aw, don't worry this is going to clear up in a couple of days.' And I said, "Man, I'm gonna make a health shake—you want one?'"

Keith just looked at him and started laughing, shaking his head and saying, "Stanley, Stanley."

COWBOY IN THE MAKING

Somewhere deep in the heart of Texas, Ronnie gets duded up with a pair of cowboy boots during a rare rest day. Henry Diltz

HORNMEN

(Opposite) Ronnie proves to one and all that he can indeed play the sax, although Bobby Keys looks dubious. Henry Diltz

CHAPTER 9
TROUBLEMAKERS

"THEY OFFER NOTHING MORE THAN EAR-TO-EAR VIOLENCE."

— NEW BARBARIANS T-SHIRT

FORT WORTH, 13 MAY 1979
The Barbarians storm Texas.
Curt Angeledes

FORT WORTH, 13 MAY 1979
(Above left and middle) The
Barbarians storm Texas. Curt Angeledes

**SALT LAKE CITY, 17 MAY
1979** (Above right) Ron slides one
on his '50s Stratocaster. Henry Diltz

**SAN DIEGO, 22 MAY
1979** (Opposite) With a halo of
spotlights behind him, Ronnie leads
the band into the last show of the
Barbarians tour. Bruce Silberman

DENVER, 15 MAY 1979 (Overleaf)
Rocking and rolling. Henry Diltz

The caravan rolled westward. After finishing out the 10 May show in Atlanta, the Barbarians boarded their 727 and choogled on down to Dallas' Fairmont Hotel to play on 12 May in Houston, the following night in Fort Worth, then on 15 May in Denver. Following the Colorado show, they shifted to their final base in Los Angeles, where Woody stayed at his home and the rest of the Barbarians set up camp at Le Parc Suites in West Hollywood to play their last four concerts: 17 May in Salt Lake City, 19 May at L.A.'s Forum, 20 May in Oakland, and the finale on 22 May in San Diego.

It was during the West Coast swing of the tour that the New Barbarians finally made a stop in a recording studio.

On 21 May, a day off, they ventured to Shangri-La Studios in Malibu to record some cuts for Ian McLagan's planned solo debut. Mac remembered in his autobiography that when the Barbarians were in Chicago, Jason Cooper got him into the Mercury Records office to arrange a deal with label president Bob Sherwood. Cooper coaxed Mercury into fronting Mac studio money, which was working its way across desks in the financial division. "But I couldn't hang around waiting for the money to come through," Mac remembered, "because I wanted to get The New Barbarians on a track before the tour finished. . . . We'd all been saying it was a shame the tour was almost over, [and] I thought this might be a way for us to get to play a little more, and for me to get a track out of it for my record at the same time.

McNichols

ARENA

The New Barbarians
McNichols Arena—Denver, Colorado
May 15, 1979

Joining fellow Barbarians Keith Richards, Ron Wood, and "friends" on this the fourteenth stop of their seventeen city tour, are the following players.
IAN McLAGAN joined the Small Faces in 1965. His organ styling was a distinctive part of the group's chartbound sound. In 1969 when the band metamorphosed into the Faces, with the addition of guitarist Ron Wood and the voice of Rod Stewart, Mac began to incorporate more piano, not only in the studio on the group's and Stewart's solo albums, but also on stage where the Faces' contract demanded a nine-foot Steinway. Always a committed band member, he rarely hired-out his sought after talents as a session player. Exceptions being at Chuck Berry's *London Sessions* lp, Ron Wood's solo albums (the second of which he co-produced), a brief tour with Mr. Bobby Womack, and a few international jaunts with the Rolling Stones.
The most influential young bassist playing today, STANLEY CLARKE'S disarming demeanor and intense approach to music, allows him the latitude and perspective to utilize an astonishing array of musical influences. In the course of the 70's Clarke has greatly expanded the role of the contemporary bass guitarist. On his own albums he functions as composer, lyricist, arranger, conductor and producer, in addition to plucking the strings on a variety of custom built basses. If tonight's association with the cream of Rock n'Roll seems slightly out-of-sync with Stanley's Return To Forever endeavors, please note that in addition to Jeff Beck and Carmine Appice, Clarke has also re-

corded with Roy Buchanan, Jeff Porcaro, Mike Garson, Jeff "Skunk" Baxter, and Aretha Franklin.
JOSEPH "ZIGGY" MODELISTE'S participation in the rich musical legacy of New Orleans, Louisiana began long before his association with the Meters. Zig Modeliste was an in demand session drummer on the New Orleans' studio scene in the early 60's. His playing enhanced Aaron Neviles' "Tell It Like It Is," Lee Dorsey's "Ya Ya," "Working In A Coal Mine," and many other recordings. Zig's an honors graduate of the ongoing musical school which has produced such luminaries as Fats Domino, Mac "Dr. John" Rebennack, Allen Toussaint, and the Neville Brothers. The Stones picked the Meters to open the first concerts on their '75 tour and summoned the band back for their 1976 swing through Europe. Along with the Meters, Modeliste has provided the okey doke for albums by Labelle, Paul McCartney's Wings, Robert Palmer, King Biscuit Boy, as well as playing on just about every Allen Toussaint produced session since 1969.
The golden saxophone of BOBBY KEYS has graced the records of "just about everyone in the business" from Yoko Ono to Buddy Holly. West Texas native, Keys recorded with Holly at K-triple-L radio, and played at the first Alan Freed Brooklyn Paramount show featuring the Everly Brothers, Clyde McPhatter and Holly's Crickets. He's toured the world with Delaney and Bonnie, Cocker's Mad Dogs and Englishmen, and the Rolling Stones.
—Radio Pete—

DENVER, 15 MAY 1979
Promotional flyer and program for the Denver show. Curt Angeledes collection

DENVER, 15 MAY 1979
(Opposite) Keith rocks the Mile-High City. Henry Diltz

"I was cautious about asking Keith to do it, because he rarely recorded with anybody other than The Stones, and I dreaded him saying 'no.' But Bobby urged me to ask him because he thought he might go for it, and when I finally plucked up the courage, I was surprised by his enthusiasm. After he was aboard, Woody, Stanley and Zig quickly said yes, too."

With time free, Mac forked out $1,000 in cash of his own money to his next-door neighbor Harold Grennell, who was part owner of Shangri-La with Rob Fraboni, and booked the studio for a day and night. "I was beginning to get a little dizzy, as it was the first time I'd ever booked a studio."

Geoff Workman, who had worked on *Gimme*, produced, with Barbarians soundman Buford T. Jones engineering. The band was filled out by Bobby Keys' brother, Darryl, on sax. Chuch, Gary Schultz, and Johnny Starbuck set up the gear "and organized the booze," as Mac said.

"Keith and Woody surprised me by arriving early. They were rested, rehearsed and ready to go, God bless 'em. Zigaboo was late,

**TROUBLEMAKER SESSIONS,
MAY 1979**
(Top) Mac directs proceedings from
behind his keyboards at Shangri-La
Studios in Malibu, California.
Henry Diltz

TROUBLEMAKER (Bottom)
McLagan's solo debut would be
released later in 1979.

which was a problem because I'd figured it might take a couple of hours to get a drum sound, but Woody jumped at the chance of playing drums, and if Zig hadn't turned up we'd still have had a decent track, because Woody can play a fair old reggae groove.

"Chuch, Gary and Johnny found some gold lamé, Parliament Funkadelic style band uniforms in a back room, and set the tone of the session by wearing them all day. Everyone was feeling good and relaxed, but in case it got too loose, Keith said, 'Come on, Mac, crack that whip. Tell us what to do, it's your session. You're the boss.'

"He was right. He knew I wasn't used to taking command, and was letting me know it was down to me to start, or it would just develop into a stoned jam. Zig arrived apologizing, and Woody got out from behind the drums, plugged his guitar in, and before you knew it we were cutting. We only ran it through for a couple of minutes before we were ready for a take. I took the intro on the piano and then everybody fell in after that. After we'd played the song through, we grooved on at the end, and eventually the headphones went dead when the tape ran out. Twelve minutes long, the basic track was done in the first take! I was over the moon with excitement, and the track sounded as good in the control room as it did in the studio.

"COME ON, MAC, CRACK THAT WHIP. TELL US WHAT TO DO, IT'S YOUR SESSION. YOU'RE THE BOSS."

— KEITH RICHARDS

TROUBLEMAKER **SESSIONS, MAY 1979** (Top left) As Ziggy was late to the session, Ronnie took over the drum kit. Mac remembers that Woody could lay down a fine "One Drop and Straight Four" reggae riddim. Henry Diltz

TROUBLEMAKER **SESSIONS, MAY 1979** (Top right) The Hard Corps— (from left) Johnny Starbuck, Chuch, and Gary Schultz—found some gold lamé outfits in a back room at Shangri-La and set the sessions' style. Remembered Mac: "Everyone was feeling good and relaxed." Henry Diltz

TROUBLEMAKER **SESSIONS, MAY 1979** (Middle and bottom) Stanley and Ziggy get down to business, setting the bottom end for Mac, while Ronnie and Keith roll out reggae riffs on "Truly." Henry Diltz

AFTERSHOW PARTY

(Top left) Following the L.A. Forum show on 19 May 1979, the Barbarians and friends retired to the Dar Maghreb Moroccan restaurant on Hollywood's Sunset Boulevard. Dave Mason does his best belly dance, while Tom Petty watches from the far corner. Keith's manager, Jane Rose, smokes a cigarette in the foreground, next to Billy Preston. Henry Diltz

AFTERSHOW PARTY

(Top right) Stanley, Billy Preston, and actor Tony Curtis share a laugh. Henry Diltz

Inset Gary Greenberg collection

"Keith bubbling on guitar, Woody jabbing and sliding, Stanley swooping up and down the neck of the bass, Zig putting fills in the most unexpected places and me thumping away like a good'un. . . . It was lots of fun, and I could have listened to the playback all night.

"But we still had a lot of work to do. Keith put another guitar on, and then he and I sang the harmonies on the choruses. Bobby and his brother Daryll, also on tenor, over-dubbed their parts and honked all the way home. We tried to get decent takes of a couple of other tunes, but when they didn't fall into place like 'Truly', we called it a night."

A couple days later, the Barbarians were in Los Angeles' RCA Studios to cut "Fingerprint Filin'" with Ziggy on vocals and Little Feat's Lowell George adding slide guitar. The finished funkified track sounded wonderfully like the Meters, and was planned as a lead cut for Ziggy's dream solo album, which never happened. Sadly, though, it would be Lowell George's last session: Just a couple days later, on 29 June, he was dead.

Later that spring, after the tour was over, Mac's sessions would continue at Cherokee Studios in L.A. with Ronnie and Bobby Keys backed by a core group made of guitarist Johnny Lee Schell, bassist Paul Stallworth, and drummer Jim Keltner. But in grand Faces style, guests appeared when guests were available, including Ringo Starr and trumpeter Steve Madaio.

Taking a hint from Schell's rocker "Little Troublemaker," Mac titled his debut *Troublemaker*, and it was released later in '79. While the album carried on the party atmosphere of the New Barbarians, only one track by the band ultimately was used—but it was one of the best. "Truly" had been cut the year prior by the Cimarons, a group

of Jamaican immigrants to England that formed the first indigenous reggae ensemble. Written by keyboardist Carl Levy, it was a sweet lilting love song, and the Barbarians reveled in that reggae riddim.

Beyond the Barbarians' "Truly," the standout track on Mac's album was without doubt his cover of Ronnie's ballad "Mystifies Me." Mac went full-on gospel with the song, his Hammond B3's Leslie swells echoed by Johnny Lee Schell's guitar lines. The outre choruses then ran over a sort of reggae backbeat punctuated by Schell's guitar stabs. The overall effect was magical. "Woody hadn't been involved in the

NEW GUITARS

During the West Coast leg of the tour, Keith and Ronnie were presented with specially made guitars by luthier Travis Bean. Henry Diltz

GUITAR TUNING ROOM

(Above and opposite) Before the shows, all of the guitars and basses were tuned up backstage. Among the arsenal were Ronnie's Buddy Emmons pedal steel; his disc-front Zemaitis that he often opened the show with, as well as two more Zemaitis guitars; Keith's Micawber; the '58 Gibson Les Paul TV Junior nicknamed "Dice"; a couple of Ronnie and Keith's early '50s Strats; and Stanley's two Alembic basses. Henry Diltz and Bruce Silberman

sessions, but he popped in when we'd finished most of the mixes. It was an opportunity to play him my version of his beautiful song 'Mystifies Me'. I hadn't told him we'd even recorded it, so it was a thrill for me to watch his reaction as Geoff cranked up the speakers and he listened to it for for the first time."

The album sold decently—"not too shabby for a beginner," Mac jested. But he was angered and embarrassed when Mercury pulled the same stunt in promoting it as Cooper had with the Barbarians tour—promoting the guest stars over the main artist. A lightning flash in the top righthand corner of the cover shouted out "Beware! There Are Some Heavyweight Musicians Playing On This Album."

Mac: "I didn't even know about it for some months, but when I found out I was really disappointed with the company and called them to complain. They told me they'd change it, but the damage was already done. If ever a record company wanted to make an artist look stupid, this was as good a way as any. It wasn't as if I'd assembled a supergroup. I'd just cut one song with the New Barbarians and Ringo had played on another, but it looked as if I'd

said: 'Forget me, look at all the famous people I know!'"

The *Troublemaker* sessions made trouble in another manner, however. As Mac remembered in his autobiography, "Bobby surprised us all when he brought out a bag of coke the size of a 'Big Mac' that some Colombian dealers had given him. But this wasn't cocaine hydrochloride. You couldn't snort it. This was base cocaine. As it wouldn't dissolve in water, you had to smoke it. It was the first time for all of us, and we smoked and played." It was the start of another era.

But that's getting ahead of things. The New Barbarians with Billy Preston as special guest played the Los Angeles Forum on

"NOT TOO SHABBY FOR A BEGINNER."

— IAN MCLAGAN

SAN DIEGO, 22 MAY 1979
(Above and opposite) Setting the stage at the San Diego Sports Arena.
Henry Diltz

Gary Greenberg collection

a Saturday night, 19 May, and everyone in the industry was there, from fellow musicians to seersucker-suited under assistant West Coast promotion men.

After the show, the party continued at the famed Dar Maghreb Moroccan restaurant on Hollywood's Sunset Boulevard. Preston, Dave Mason, Jason Cooper, actor Tony Curtis, and the whole crew were there. Fernandez: "I remember that Elliot Roberts had just got a new act, Tom Petty. I invited them down to show and introduced them to Keith and Woody and after the show, we all had dinner." The restaurant featured a large central fountain, and Stanley remembered that by the night's end, most everyone ended up wet.

For Keith, though, the L.A. stop was a setback. Lil Wergilis' mother was taken ill and she flew back to Sweden to be with her. "And I had a temporary lapse in her absence. I bought some Persian brown from a woman named Cathy Smith in Los Angeles. I described myself at the time as 'reliving a second rock-and-roll childhood.' Cathy Smith was also the downfall of Belushi. It was just

too strong for Belushi. Basically he was a very strong bloke, but he just pushed it over the limit."

Just before the 22 May finale in San Diego with special guest Bob Welch, two would-be filmmakers approached Ronnie about videotaping the concert for a movie. They didn't yet have funding for the film, but that would come later, they promised—or at least, hoped. Ken Graham worked with them, boosting lightning levels on stage to aid the filming.

To fill out the planned movie, the duo would later film the Barbarians at the Knebworth Festival. It was a last-minute deal, Graham remembers, and he helped organize the filming while a friend took over running the Barbarians' production and lighting for that show. Afterwards, Graham took care of bringing the video back to Malibu. "I remember buying this heavy-duty suitcase and all the raw video tape got put into that suitcase. I brought it back through customs and went out to the West Coast and gave it to these guys, who were going to raise the money to put out the film—and that's the last I've heard of it."

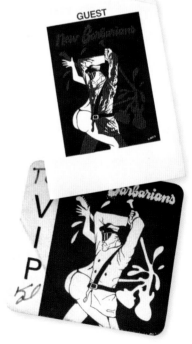

Gary Greenberg collection

During these last shows, the Barbarians were a well-oiled band. *Melody Maker* writer Mark Williams waxed poetic about the San Diego show. Opening as usual with "Sweet Little Rock & Roller," the Barbarians commenced proceedings with a "jack-hammer urgency they never bettered later" in the show, he said. Keith "delivered regular bursts of stunning guitaring undertaken with admirable athletic zeal. If it's *de rigeur* to say that he looked fitter and healthier than he's ever done, then I will . . . but my abiding image of the man is that he looked more like Nils Lofgren than Nils Lofgren." And Keys blew his tenor "with a venom that had you waiting anxiously for the sax break on every one of the set's 20 numbers. Thank God for Bobby Keys." Ziggy and Stanley were a "super-tight and occasionally riveting black rhythm section," and Williams exited the show with "an unanticipated admiration for Stanley Clarke—how many times have you seen an audience on its feet for a bass guitar solo?"

And yet the Barbarians' final show was also upset by a disturbance in the crowd. According to reports, an overzealous—or maybe

SAN DIEGO, 22 MAY 1979

(Top and opposite) As Ronnie told *Creem* about his role as frontman, "I just imagine I'm filling in for Mick all the time." Bruce Silberman and Henry Diltz

Inset Gary Greenberg collection

SAN DIEGO, 22 MAY 1979
(Above left) Keith sports his red-leather pants bearing the initials "J.H." on the leg: "These are Jimi Hendrix's old pants," he told photographer Bruce Silberman. Bruce Silberman

SAN DIEGO, 22 MAY 1979
(Above right) To the last, Stanley and Ziggy's solo slot was a musical highpoint of the show. Henry Diltz

SAN DIEGO, 22 MAY 1979
(Opposite) The Barbarians' string section. Henry Diltz

SAN DIEGO, 22 MAY 1979
(Overleaf) Rocking in style. Curt Angeledes

overly amped-up fan—knocked down a woman who was on crutches, sparking the surrounding audience to chastise the fan. Both Keith and Ronnie witnessed the fracas from onstage. Keith yanked off his Telecaster as if he was going to use it as a weapon, yelling to Barbarians security man Big Jim Callahan, "J.C., get that bleeder before I kill him!" As the fan exited, a furious Ronnie interrupted his interrupted solo to bless the guy with an upright middle finger.

With the Barbarians' tour at an end, it was time at last to rest. The band and crew retired to Palm Springs and the Two Bunch Palms resort. Established in the 1940s, the resort had reputedly been gangster Al Capone's West Coast hideout when the heat got too close; it later served as a discreet hideaway for Hollywood celebrities. The original central house was built around a central corridor with rooms on each side, each with an escape door outside for gangster's getaways. Up in the attic were windows with the odd measurements of two feet high by eight inch wide—"No, they weren't windows; they

SAN DIEGO, 22 MAY 1979
The Barbarians strut their stuff
during the tour's final show. Bruce
Silberman

"THANK GOD FOR BOBBY KEYS."

— *MELODY MAKER*

SAN DIEGO, 22 MAY 1979
Ronnie plays for the audience.
Curt Angeledes

SAN DIEGO, 22 MAY 1979
(Above) Keith hits a high note on Micawber. Henry Diltz

SAN DIEGO, 22 MAY 1979
Brothers in arms: Ronnie and Keith went together like drunk and disorderly. Henry Diltz

were *gunsights*!" Graham says. "They always had guys up in the roof keeping lookout."

Two Bunch Palms was built around a hot springs rich in the restorative mineral lithium that neighbored a stream ideal for cooling off: natural swimming pools and jacuzzis abounded, and there was even a small waterfall to bathe in. And there was once a casino, now shut down. Ronnie and Jo took over a townhouse; Keith and Lil had another. "We just chilled out," Gary Schultz remembers.

"It was all very low key," Graham adds. "Keith would come up with the menu for the day. The handyman would go get groceries, I collected wood for the firepit, and Keith did a lot of the grilling—hamburgers, hot dogs, steaks, chicken, salads. There was a big stone patio that we hung out on, smoking, drinking, always barefoot, reggae music playing all the time."

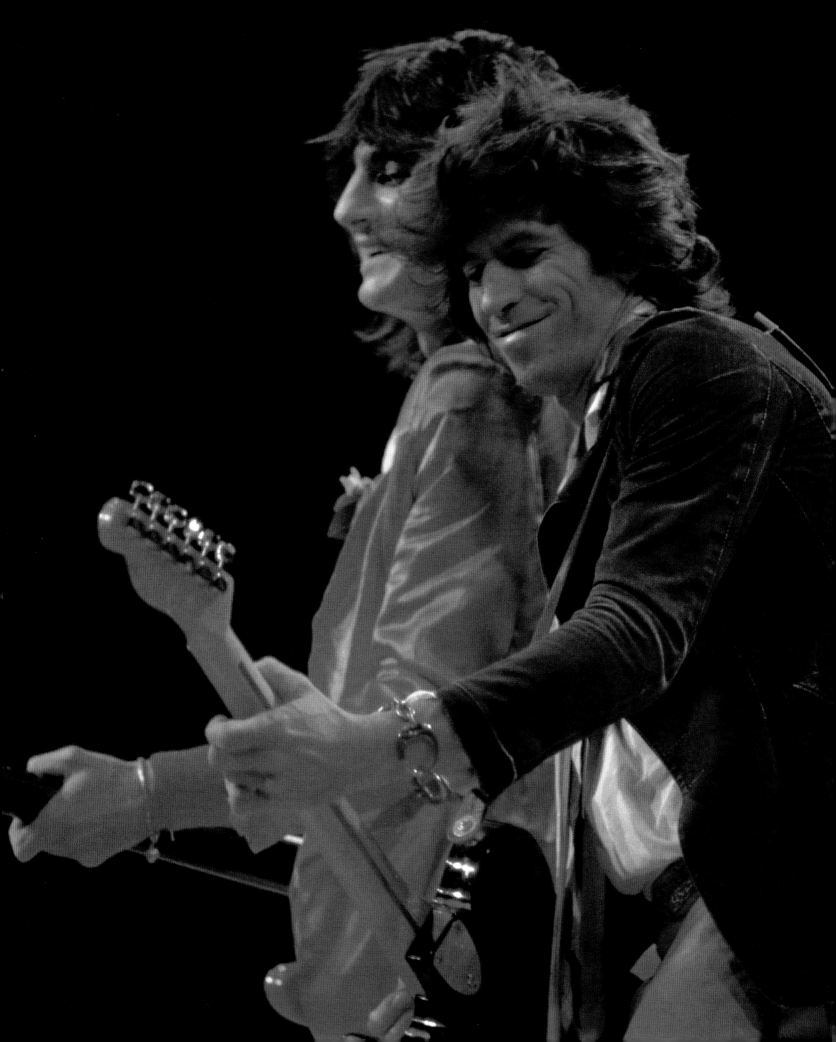

CHAPTER 10

ENCORE

"KEITH RICHARDS DIDN'T FALL OVER, HE DRANK JACK DANIELS STRAIGHT FROM THE BOTTLE AND HIS SHOELACES WERE PINK."

— **PETER SILVERTON**
REPORTING ON THE KNEBWORTH FESTIVAL, *SOUNDS*

KNEBWORTH FESTIVAL, 11 AUGUST 1979
(Opposite) Ronnie Wood and Keith Richards lead the Barbarians' attack.
Graham Wiltshire/REX/Shutterstock

Inset Voyageur Press collection

**KNEBWORTH FESTIVAL,
11 AUGUST 1979**

Ronnie—with Barbarians hydration
in hand—backstage before the band's
show. Mirrorpix

Later in the summer of '79, Ronnie was on the phone again: He had an opportunity for the New Barbarians to regroup and play one more gig. England's premier open-air pop festival, the Knebworth Festival, had come calling. The Barbarians were invited to open for Led Zeppelin.

Knebworth Festival was held on the grounds of the Tudor Gothic Knebworth Manor House in Hertfordshire, just north of London. Open-air festivals had been held in Knebworth Park since 1974.

The festival was founded by veteran rock promoter Freddy Bannister, who had earlier started the Bath Festival of Blues. Over the years, Bannister had booked some of the biggest names in rock to headline his Knebworth events: the Allman Brothers in '74, Pink Floyd in '75, the Rolling Stones and Lynyrd Skynyrd in '76, Genesis in '77, and Frank Zappa in '78. Now, it was to be Led Zeppelin in '79. (And, unbeknownst to all, it would be Zeppelin's last U.K. show before the death of drummer John Bonham just months later.)

The festival ran two, non-consecutive days in 1979, both head-lined by Led Zeppelin. On 4 August, the rest of the lineup included Todd Rundgren's Utopia, Southside Johnny and the Asbury Jukes, the New Commander Cody Band, Fairport Convention, Chas and Dave. The New Barbarians were added to the 11 August show. Listed on posters for the festival was the Marshall Tucker Band, who ultimately didn't appear.

KNEBWORTH FESTIVAL, 11 AUGUST 1979
(Left) Dragging his black-velvet jacket in the dust, Keith makes his entrance in the backstage area before the Barbarians' show. Monitor engineer Dave "Snake" Reynolds brings up the rear in his Showco T-shirt. Mirrorpix

KNEBWORTH FESTIVAL, 21 AUGUST 1976
(Overleaf) Knebworth attracted a Woodstock-like crowd of topless hippies, rude boys, and Sex Pistol–era punkers that stretched to the horizon. The Stones played the festival in 1976, three years before the Barbarians took the stage. Keystone/Hulton Archive/Getty Images

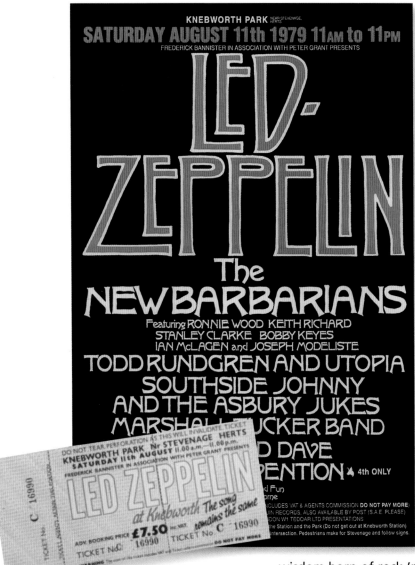

(Poster text:)

KNEBWORTH PARK NEAR STEVENAGE. HERTS
SATURDAY AUGUST 11th 1979 11AM to 11PM
FREDERICK BANNISTER IN ASSOCIATION WITH PETER GRANT PRESENTS
LED-ZEPPELIN
The NEW BARBARIANS
Featuring RONNIE WOOD KEITH RICHARD
STANLEY CLARKE BOBBY KEYES
IAN McLAGEN and JOSEPH MODELISTE
TODD RUNDGREN AND UTOPIA
SOUTHSIDE JOHNNY
AND THE ASBURY JUKES
MARSHALL TUCKER BAND
...D DAVE
...ENTION 4th ONLY

(Ticket text:)
DO NOT TEAR PERFORATION AS THIS WILL INVALIDATE TICKET
KNEBWORTH PARK Nr STEVENAGE HERTS
SATURDAY 11th AUGUST 11.00 a.m.—11.00 p.m.
FREDERICK BANNISTER IN ASSOCIATION WITH PETER GRANT PRESENTS
LED ZEPPELIN
at Knebworth The song remains the same
ADV. BOOKING PRICE £7.50 INC. VAT.
TICKET No. 16990 TICKET No C · 16990
TICKET No: C · 16990

KNEBWORTH FESTIVAL, 11 AUGUST 1979

(Top) Festival poster. Voyageur Press collection

KNEBWORTH FESTIVAL, 11 AUGUST 1979

(Bottom) Entry ticket. Matt Lee collection

KNEBWORTH FESTIVAL, 11 AUGUST 1979

(Opposite) Keith and the Barbarians play for the largest crowd of the band's short career, opening for Led Zeppelin. Andre Csillag/REX/Shutterstock

The Barbarians reunited on 10 August at Shepperton Studios, a film studio in Shepperton, Surrey. As with the Culver Studios, this offered a full soundstage for the crew to set up the gear. Ronnie was there, along with Keith, Mac, Bobby Keys, and Ziggy. Stanley was committed elsewhere, so Mac's old friend Phil Chen took his place. Chen was a Jamaican of Chinese ancestry with a mile-long résumé in ska and reggae bands starting with the Presidents, the Vikings, Jimmy James and the Vagabonds, Desmond Dekker, Jimmy Cliff, and Bob Marley; he had recently backed Jeff Beck on *Blow by Blow*. The Barbarians worked their usual rehearsal—half party, half business—and they were ready. Phil Chen learned all of the twelve-song songlist in one day.

Come 6:30 p.m. on 11 August—their scheduled start time at Knebworth—the Barbarians were nowhere to be found, however. Thirty minutes later, an hour, ninety minutes, and the stage was still empty.

The problem was the money. With wisdom born of rock 'n' roll experience, Ronnie refused to lead the band onstage until they had been paid. And here begins one of the more amazing stories of the Barbarians' career.

Bruce Silberman was heir to a parking-lot empire, not something to be sneezed at in the automobile-centric world of Southern California. But as kids are wont to do at any time and age, but especially in the '70s, he decided to take a break from the family business and become a rock 'n' roll photographer. He was pals with Chuch Magee, and Chuch invited him to come along to be the Barbarians' official photographer at Knebworth. Silberman bought a plane ticket to London, hung out with the band, and shot them during rehearsals. Come the day of the show, the Barbarians were encamped in the Montcalm Hotel in London with Ronnie's barrister, Barry Ross, trying to negotiate by phone with Knebworth promoter Freddy Bannister to get their money in hand before they'd go on. "Apparently they

were concerned about *ever* getting paid—they found the dealing unsavory," Silberman remembers. But payment remained just a promise, so the Barbarians weren't budging.

Chuch then pushed Silberman forward, explaining to Ronnie and Co. that he had experience with parking-lot contracts, real estate negotiations, and assorted other types of handy business acumen. He was just the man they needed. So Silberman unpacked his camera bag—his grandfather's olive-drab canvas World War I U.S. Army radio pack—and set forth.

"I went out to Knebworth to the management office, which was a makeshift building on stilts at the back, and I said, 'I'm here to collect the Barbarians' money. The band said they will not play until I collect their £35,000.' Now the crowd was *big*—50,000 or 80,000 (no one in fact knew for sure *how* big it was). And they had been waiting for the Barbarians: They were pushing toward the stage, they were agitated, throwing things, getting unruly. And the promoter was real argumentative; he wouldn't pay. So I said, 'Let the crowd go nuts, 'cause the Barbarians aren't coming until I call them and tell them I have their money.' And that crowd was getting wilder and angrier. Finally, he handed me the cash—a *lot* of cash—and I packed it into my old army bag and left.

Silberman drove back to the Barbarians' hotel and asked the hotel manager to put the money in the safe. The manager told him that the rooms had safety-deposit boxes, but Silberman was smart: "I wanted to put it in the hotel's safe, so they'd have to count it and give me a receipt for it. If I put it in my room's safety-deposit box, someone could later claim that it wasn't all there and we'd have no proof." So the manager duly counted the £35,000 and gave him a receipt. Silberman then called the band, who were in limousines with a car phone parked within the festival grounds, and the Barbarians hit the stage, fashionably late.

That Ronnie Wood and Co. were wise to wait on their monies before playing at Knebworth was borne out—by the fate of the festival's promotion company itself. No one knew for sure how large the crowds were at the two days of the Knebworth Festival, facts that became the source of a later legal dispute brought against Freddy Bannister's concert-promotion company, Tredoar, by Led Zeppelin and their manager, Peter Grant, concerning the band's percentage of the gate. The suit would force Tredoar into bankruptcy and thus end the festival after the 1980 edition.

Once they were finally onstage, Ronnie began by apologizing for the band's tardiness, saying, "Sorry you've had to wait, but there's

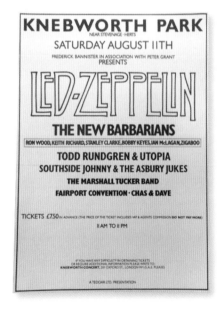

KNEBWORTH FESTIVAL, 11 AUGUST 1979
Flyer advertising the show.

Matt Lee collection

"SORRY YOU'VE HAD TO WAIT, BUT THERE'S BEEN A FEW . . . ER . . . TECHNICAL HITCHES."

— RONNIE WOOD

been a few . . . *er* . . . technical hitches." That moment would later be carefully excised from the official released videos.

Then, without hesitation, Woody laid into "Sweet Little Rock & Roller," almost before the rest of the band was ready. But by the end of the first verse, they had their groove back. "Ronnie skips around like someone's just stuffed a large handful of Mexican jumping beans down his rock and roll tight trousers while Keith gets straight down to business," reported *Sounds* magazine.

By the second tune—"F.U.C. Her"—the Barbarians were going strong. Ronnie, dressed in a blood-red jacket, wailed a solo on his '55 Strat. Then Keith, resplendent in a black-velvet coat that he wore suitably déshabillé, took over with his color-coordinated black-on-black '75 Telecaster Custom. Bobby Keys followed, blowing his sax as if his life depended on it. The Woodstockian sea of topless hippies, rude boys, and punkers that had been throwing anything worth throwing at the crew in their impatience, immediately forgave the Barbarians and began cutting some serious rug.

The Barbarians played only twelve numbers, filled out by harmonica player Sugar Blue (a.k.a James Whiting), who had played on "Miss You." Sugar Blue added his harp to "I Can Feel The Fire" and "Worried Life Blues." *Sounds* said that "'Before They Make Me Run' is just as it should be—a mixture of self-pity, bottle, pain, white powders, Jack Daniels and loose-limbed chords lobbed around like a football on a sunny afternoon kickabout in the park."

When the Barbarians hit the last notes of "Jumpin' Jack Flash," they were no more.

KNEBWORTH FESTIVAL, 11 AUGUST 1979
(Overleaf)Last hurrah: Ronnie and Keith trade licks. Keith's mum, Doris Richards, was at the Knebworth show with his children, Marlon and Dandelion. As she told Barbara Charone, "I wanted to shout to everyone, 'That's my son up there!' I'm so proud." Andre Csillag/REX/Shutterstock

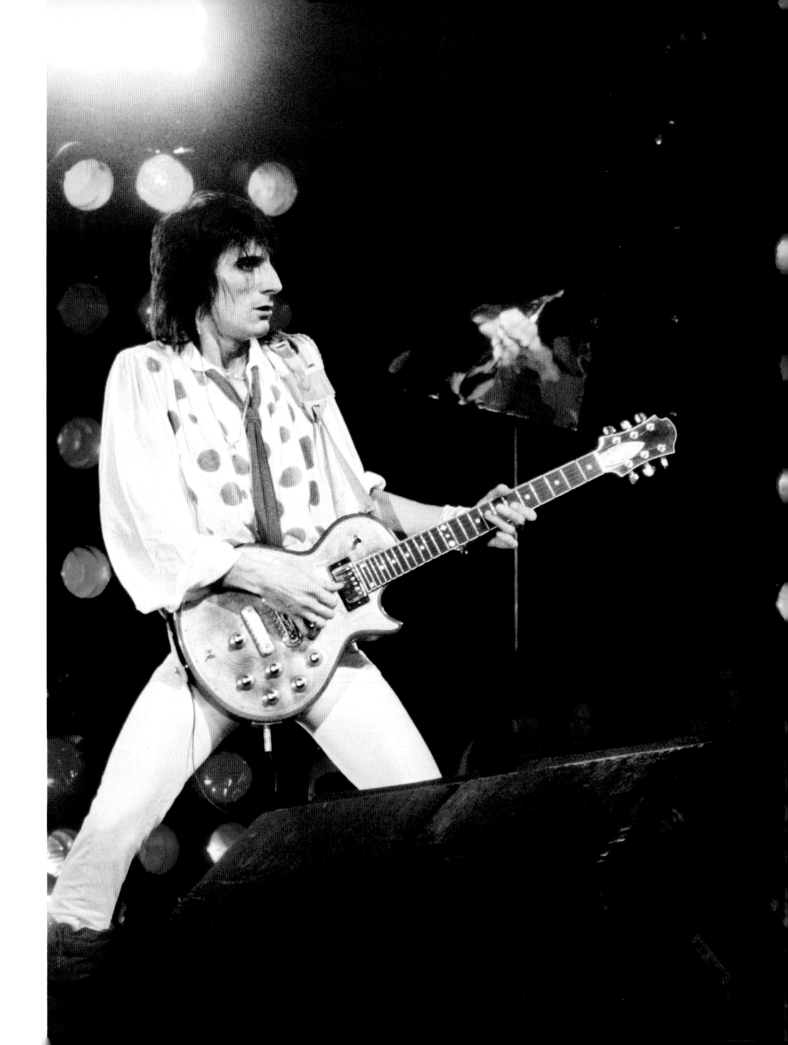

FINALE

"I CAN'T EVEN REMEMBER MUCH OF IT, IT WAS SO MUCH FUN."

— KEITH RICHARDS

The New Barbarians' music wasn't rocket science—it was just good old, unapologetic, moneymaker-shaking, 200-proof rock 'n' roll. Looking back, the band may have been just a footnote to rock 'n' roll and Rolling Stones history, but they were a footnote vibrating with great music. Their legacy of bootlegged recordings and filmed moments onstage is sparse; they were a flash in the pan, but they were a glorious one.

At the time, a chorus of critics challenged the band's merits. Many fell into the trap of missing the simple brilliance of the Barbarians while pondering, *What could have been—if only Rod or Mick were there too . . . ?*

Many concert reviews harped on the lack of Big Names. *Sounds* magazine was typical: "To cut it in the big American stadia you need more than a massive PA system that'll transmit a roadie's fart half a mile on a windless night or a brilliantly lit stage set in blood-red drapes and scarlet speaker enclosures, and you need more than a well-oiled rock machine comprised of the best back-up men money can buy. In the 14,000-seat Forum you need a sense of purpose, and to me that's what they lacked." What they needed, according to the reviewer, was a "convincing" frontman—Mick Jagger or Rod Stewart. "Everyone else seemed to get enjoyment from the whole event, however, including those massed on stage. But I guess I was using the Stones and the Faces as yardsticks – and those are pretty hard sticks to beat."

Talk about being crowned with a spike right through their heads.

Others, though, got it. Charles Shaar Murray, one of the sharpest—and sharpest-witted—rock critics ever, wrote in *New Musical Express*: "The New Barbarians show is rough, warm, human, good-humoured, energetic, unassuming and strictly life-size. When you see it, you ain't staring at something gigantic and far away. It's not as spectacular and legend-soaked as a Stones show, but it has a warmth and humanity and friendliness that will never waft off a stage that has Mick Jagger on it and THE ROLLING STONES on the poster outside. Whether you still believe in the great Stones myth of The Greatest Rock And Roll Band In The World or whether you see them in the post-punk light as a bunch of poncy smacked-back old jackoffs, they can never be just a rock band playing for your pleasure and theirs. The New Barbarians can. That's the difference."

And Robert Duncan in *Creem* understood it as well: "There were no great highlights, except for the music itself—rock 'n' roll. Which for a change, no one interfered with. In other words, the shows were great the way a good, cheap meal in an out-of-the-way roadhouse is great: satisfying, with no Mick Jagger added, fulfilling something in your gut that needs loud music and overwhelming rhythm to stay healthy and happy. The New Barbarians are—or *were*, I'm afraid, by the time you read this—a rock 'n' roll band with no superlatives and no equivocations and that was the highlight: seeing unadorned rock 'n' roll played just as it should be."

But there was more to the band's legacy. Something deeper. The New Barbarians—Ronnie's simple pickup band—played a key, if unsung and under-recognized, role in the history of the Stones. That of deliverance.

Keith's Toronto heroin bust of early '77 was one of the band's nadirs, threatening its very survival. His lost years that followed turned his life around: kicking the poppy addiction; leaving behind his *éminence blonde*, Anita Pallenberg; and meeting, in March 1979, a young model named Patti Hansen, who'd later become his wife. Finally, he seemed to find true joy again in playing rock 'n' roll while he was part of the New Barbarians. So, if there's ever doubt about the importance of the band, just let Keith have his say: "The Barbarians in a weird fucking way saved my life."

True, at the end of the Barbarians' tour during the *Troublemaker* sessions, both Ronnie and Bobby Keys were introduced to freebase cocaine, which they met with a hearty handshake and would ultimate devour too many years of their lives. But their time would come—just as it did for Keith Richards.

The Barbarians themselves knew they were making history—or if not, at least great music. Tour manager Richard Fernandez was still gushing about the band decades later: "Maybe it didn't sell 85 million records and make a ton of money, but just the vibe and seeing these cats and who they were and how they treated each other, it was really special shit."

Ian McLagan, ever the playful poet, told *Creem*, "If variety's the spice of life . . . then play on. I love it. It's the happiest band I've ever been in."

With Texas-sized braggadocio, Bobby Keys boasted, "We are the only band that has ever sold out Madison Square Garden *and* the Los Angeles Forum without having a record on the street."

And as usual, Zigaboo Modeliste summed up simply and succinctly: "This band had a special meaning."

Ronnie Wood deserves the final word, of course: "You know what, in the name of great music, I'd do it again and wouldn't change a thing."

ACKNOWLEDGMENTS

Over the course of compiling this book, we were fortunate to talk with many of the people involved in the New Barbarians. We extend our thanks to Ronnie Wood, Keith Richards, Ian McLagan, Bobby Keys, Stanley Clarke, and Ziggy Modeliste. Thanks as well to new New Barbarians Johnny Lee Schell and Phil Chen.

And this book—like the Barbarians themselves—never would have happened without the help of the managers, crew, and studio folks; our thanks to Richard Fernandez, Ken Graham, Gary Schultz, Johnny Starbuck, Ernie Selgado, and Rob Fraboni.

We also thank others involved with Barbarians: Henry Diltz, Bruce Silberman, and Barbarians travel agent Brooks Ogden, as well as Jane Rose and Sherry Daly.

Our further thanks to the following people who helped in myriad ways, listed here in alphabetical order: Richard Aaron, Robert Alford, Curt Angeledes, Geoff Gans, Gary Greenberg, Matt Lee, Robert Matheu, Barbara Pariser, Michael Putland, Ebet Roberts, and everyone at Quarto and Voyageur Press.

Finally, a huge thanks to Dennis Pernu, for his usual wisdom; and for her inestimable knowledge and help, Sherill Pociecha.

Many thanks and deep gratitude to two cool cats, Danny Beck and Johnny Clifford.

INDEX

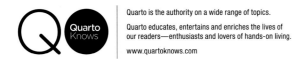

Quarto is the authority on a wide range of topics.

Quarto educates, entertains and enriches the lives of our readers—enthusiasts and lovers of hands-on living.

www.quartoknows.com

First published in 2016 by Voyageur Press, an imprint of Quarto Publishing Group USA Inc., 400 First Avenue North, Suite 400, Minneapolis, MN 55401 USA.
Telephone: (612) 344-8100 Fax: (612) 344-8692

quartoknows.com
Visit our blogs at quartoknows.com

Voyageur Press titles are also available at discounts in bulk quantity for industrial or sales-promotional use. For details contact the Special Sales Manager at Quarto Publishing Group USA Inc., 400 First Avenue North, Suite 400, Minneapolis, MN 55401 USA.

10 9 8 7 6 5 4 3 2

ISBN: 978-0-7603-5014-0

Library of Congress Control Number: 2016946692

Art Direction and Cover Design: Cindy Samargia Laun
Book Design and Layout: Ashley Prine, Tandem Books

On the front cover: Photo by Bruce Silberman
On the back cover: Illustration by Ron Wood
On the frontis: *Gimme Some Neck wooden* coin courtesy Curt Angeledes; **Keith Richards pin** courtesy Gary Greenberg; backstage pass Voyageur Press collection; **New Barbarians on stage in San Diego** Curt Angeledes
On page 4: New Barbarian concert tickets. Curt Angeledes, Gary Greenberg, and Voyageur Press collections
On page 5: Ronnie Wood's drawing of himself from the *Gimme Some Neck* promotional package. Voyageur Press collection
On page 6: Ronnie Wood and Keith Richards front the New Barbarians at their final, San Diego show. Curt Angeledes
On the title page: Keith Richards pin Michael Dregni collection; **New Barbarians passes** Gary Greenberg collection
On the contents page: Chief Barbarians. Henry Diltz

Printed in China

MIX
Paper from responsible sources
FSC
www.fsc.org   FSC® C016973